THE SAGA OF LARTEN CREPSLEY

THE SAGA OF LARTEN CREPSLEY

PALACE OF THE DAMNED

DARREN SHAN

LITTLE, BROWN AND COMPANY

New York Boston

Copyright © 2011 by Darren Shan

Little, Brown and Company

Hachette Book Group
237 Park Avenue, New York, NY 10017
Visit our website at www.lb-teens.com

Little, Brown and Company is a division of Hachette Book Group, Inc.
The Little, Brown name and logo are trademarks of Hachette Book Group, Inc.

The publisher is not responsible for websites (or their content)
that are not owned by the publisher.

First U.S. Paperback Edition: October 2012
First U.S. hardcover edition published in October 2011 by Little, Brown and Company
First published in Great Britain by Collins in 2011

Library of Congress Cataloging-in-Publication Data
Shan, Darren.
  Palace of the damned / by Darren Shan. —1st U.S. ed.
    p. cm. — (The saga of Larten Crepsley ; [3])
  Prequel to Cirque Du Freak series.
  Summary: Having received a sign that he is not meant to die, young vampire Larten tries to live in the human world, raising the infant who survived his vengeful killing of a ship's crew and falling in love with a human girl, but the darkness inside him forces him back to Vampire Mountain.
  ISBN 978-0-316-07870-2 (hc) / ISBN 978-0-316-07869-6 (pb)
  [1. Vampires—Fiction. 2. Horror stories.] 1. Title.
PZ7.S52823Pal 2011
[Fic]—dc22

2011009716

10 9 8 7 6 5 4 3 2 1

RRD-C

Printed in the United States of America

Part One

"a palace of the dead"

Chapter One

A huffing Larten Crepsley mounted a treacherous, icy ridge and stared across a frozen sea of jagged peaks. He had visited most parts of the world in his decades as a vampire, but this was the harshest wilderness he'd ever experienced. A plateau of ice peppered with rocky outcrops. Whipping snow that could blind a man in minutes. Temperatures so low that each breath stung his throat and lungs. It was a hostile, alien, unforgiving landscape.

Larten threw back his head and howled with mad delight. He was loving this! There was no better place for a vampire to perish than in an area where no human would dare tread. This would make for a brutal, lonely death, and he deserved nothing better. A fitting end for a savage killer.

The baby he was carrying moaned softly and shivered beneath the covering of the vampire's shirt. Larten was holding him clasped in one arm, sheltered from the wind and snow as much as possible. He felt a stab of guilt at the baby's cry and paused to puff a breath of warm air down the neck of his shirt. The boy gurgled happily, then shivered again.

Larten wished he'd left the baby behind. Taking him was an act of madness. He had done it to save the child from a cannibal, but he saw now how crazy he'd been. The boy had stood a chance on the ship, but was doomed for sure out here in this chilling realm of death.

"At least you will find Paradise," Larten whispered, rubbing the baby's back to keep him warm. "And my soul will not be there to trouble you."

Every vampire dreamed of going to Paradise when he died. It was the reward at the end of the road to which every night-walker aspired. But Larten was sure he would never know that eternal peace. He had lost his mind on the ship and slaughtered the crew and passengers, including the baby's parents. True, they had hung an innocent girl – poor, loyal Malora –

but they'd thought she was a monster. ("Like me," Larten croaked.) Their punishment far outweighed their crime.

A cruel wind cut through Larten and he staggered down the other side of the ridge. He had lost track of time in this barren land of ice. It felt like he had been wandering for days, but he suspected it was more like twelve hours. A vampire could survive a long time in conditions like these, but a human baby? Larten guessed the boy was close to the limits of his fragile form.

He considered backtracking, to return the baby to the ship, but he'd lost his way many hours earlier. Everything looked the same once you got away from the coast. He wouldn't be able to find the rowboat again. Even if he did, the ship would have sailed on, and Larten had no idea in which direction the towns lay.

Towns! It was hard to believe anyone could live here, but there were areas along the coast where life was supported. If Larten knew how to find them, he would have taken the baby to the nearest homestead and left him to the mercy of the people within. But the towns could be anywhere. It was impossible to judge.

"You will have to die with me," he mumbled, teeth chattering, orange hair caked with frost, eyes slit against the wind and snow. "But we will find a good place to perish. I can do that much right at least."

Larten's only concern now was to find a cave that could serve as the baby's tomb. Larten didn't care if he himself died in the open, to be buried in snow or torn apart by scavengers. But he wanted something better for the boy, a sheltered, quiet place where his remains wouldn't be disturbed.

The wind roared around them and the temperature dropped. Larten hadn't thought it could get any colder, but he was wrong. Even his vampire blood seemed poised to turn to ice in his veins. His exposed flesh was numb. His lips were drawn back from his teeth in a grimace. The scar on the left side of his face was blue from the chill. Only his chest was marginally warm, where the baby nestled beneath his shirt.

Larten slipped and almost collapsed on top of the boy, but managed to twist and fall on his side. He gasped from the shock of the cold impact. Part of him wanted to lie there and let nature take its course. If he had been alone, he might have stopped. It would have been easier than rising and pushing on. But there was the baby to consider, so he prepared himself to get up.

As he struggled to his feet, he caught sight of something pounding towards him. It was massive, white like the snow, almost invisible. If not for its dark eyes he would have missed it until it was upon him. He had seen polar bears before, but even if he hadn't, he would have known this beast instantly. In the wastelands of the north, what else could it be?

Larten tore his shirt open, dropped the startled baby and leaped forward. The bear was female, not as large as some he'd seen, but still taller than Larten when erect. She looked scraggly and starved. An elderly sow, well past her prime. She had been tracking Larten for an hour. A more cunning creature would have waited even longer, until her prey was too weak to defend himself. But when she saw the man slip, her mouth watered and she could hold back no longer.

Larten threw himself at the bear as she reared up on two legs and bellowed at him. He was in worse shape than the sow, but he had a child to protect and that gave him a slight, desperate edge. He didn't care what happened to him, but he wasn't going to let this ferocious carnivore feast on the hot, steaming innards of the baby.

As the bear wrapped her limbs around Larten, he

dug for her eyes with his thumbs. All vampires had hard, sharp nails, but Larten's were longer and more jagged than usual, since he hadn't trimmed them while suffering with a fever on the ship. The nail on his left thumb found the bear's eye and speared it at the first attempt.

The sow yowled and shook her head, snapping at Larten's arm. She had endured much pain in her time, but nothing like this. She had already forgotten the promise of food. All she cared about now was killing the brute who had hurt her.

Larten couldn't afford a drawn-out fight. He knew that even with one eye the bear would soon wear him down if he tried to spar with her. If he didn't finish her swiftly, he would die, and the baby too.

Ignoring the threat of the gnashing fangs, Larten dug the nails of his right hand into the bear's neck. The fur was thick and the skin was tough, but Larten pierced both coverings and his nails sank into hot flesh and drew blood.

As the sow howled and clawed at his back, Larten grabbed the fur on the other side of the beast's neck and pulled so that the skin beneath was stretched tight. Opening his mouth wide, he latched on to her throat and bit hard. He worked his teeth savagely from side to side, biting and chewing, ignoring the pain as the bear's claws cut deep into his back. Blood shot up his nose and he almost choked. But he snorted it out and jammed his chin in farther, sliding his lower teeth left and right like a saw.

The bear spewed blood and her grip slackened. But Larten didn't relax — he wasn't going to fall into the same trap that she had when she saw him topple. He continued to chew until the sow collapsed, convulsed a few times and fell still.

When it was over, Larten rolled aside, panting, warm for the first time since he'd stepped ashore. His eyes were bright and he was grinning horribly. He was going to die in this godsforsaken land, but at least he'd squeezed in one last, decent fight. It was a pity the bear hadn't been younger and stronger — this would have been a good way to perish. Perhaps he could find another to finish the job.

The baby cried out weakly, reminding Larten that he wasn't alone and hadn't just his own fate to consider. He could track down a fiercer bear later. First he had to deal with the baby and find a final resting place for the boy, somewhere safe from the creatures that would otherwise pick his bones clean.

Larten crawled across and picked up the trembling

child. As he settled the baby back inside his shirt, he paused and glanced at the dead polar bear. He was keen to press on, but there was no telling how long it might take to find a cave. If he fell before he laid the boy to rest, he'd fail in his quest to secure the baby a tomb. It was a pointless quest but Larten had fixed on the idea. He had done much wrong in his life, but he didn't want to add to the list at this late stage. Finding a cave where he could lay the child's remains wouldn't change anything in the grand scheme of things, but it mattered to Larten. In that land of the lost, it was all that he cared about.

Larten scratched at his injured back – the wounds were deep, but not life-threatening – while considering his course. He could dig through the fur and flesh of the bear's stomach with his nails. There would be hot juices inside. Digested food that he could mash up and feed to the baby. It would make for a foul meal, but the boy wouldn't complain once his stomach was full. And Larten could fashion wraps out of the fur, one for the child and another for himself. Protected and fed, they could maybe march for another day or two. Surely that would give him all the time he needed to find a cave for his young, doomed charge.

Grimacing against the pain in his back, Larten

wiped blood from his lips and knelt by the bear. He said a quick prayer over its carcass, then made a blade of his fingers and set to work, staying hunched against the snow that never stopped blowing while he sliced open the dead bear's stomach and trawled through a maze of steaming, gooey guts.

Chapter Two

A storm was raging. It had whipped up without warning and had been blowing for hours. Larten struggled through it, his face buried in the rough cloak he'd made from the fur of the polar bear. The baby was covered entirely and was gurgling happily in the dark, sticky warmth.

Larten had slipped many times and almost fallen through cracks in the ice. This was deadly land if you couldn't see clearly. Very easy to wander off the edge of a ridge or drop into an icy abyss. It would have been best to sit, covered by the fur, and wait out the storm.

But the baby would soon be hungry again. Larten had brought some strips of meat, which he could chew up and feed to the child like a bird feeding a chick. But he didn't know if the boy would be able to stomach such an offering. He hadn't reacted favorably to yesterday's foul feast and had vomited up most of it. Larten was resigned to the fact that the baby would die, but he hated the thought of the infant starving to death in his arms. So he pushed on, preferring the idea of the baby falling into a chasm with him to perishing of hunger.

Larten pictured faces of the dead as he stumbled forward. Vur Horston, Traz, Wester's family, Zula Pone and of course the faces of the people on the ship, the doomed crew and passengers, fresh in his memory and with more cause than the others to haunt his thoughts.

But mostly he found himself focusing on the face of poor Malora, filling with guilt and regret when he recalled how she had died protecting him and how he had failed her in her hour of need. He would never forgive himself for not being there when she had needed him most.

Seba had said, many years ago before blooding him, that a vampire had to prepare himself for a lifetime of death. When you lived as long as they did, most of the people you knew would die before you.

Larten had accepted that. He wasn't afraid of death or the grief he must endure when losing a loved one. That was the way of the clan and he faced the hardships without complaint.

But in that icy wilderness, his mind still askew from the madness that had consumed him on the ship, Larten cursed his long years and the choices he'd made. He felt that the dead were jealous of him, that they hated him for being alive. He cringed as he imagined their voices on the wind, their hands snaking around his ankles, an army of ghosts rising up to drag him down and torment him.

Something shimmered far off to his right. Larten thought his mind was playing tricks but then it came again, a flash of yellow and green. He stopped and squinted. The snow was thick as ever and it was almost impossible to see anything farther than a couple of feet away. But Larten held his position and kept his eyes open. Moments later the flicker of colors came again, but farther off this time.

Larten didn't know what it might be. An animal? He couldn't think of any green or yellow animals in this part of the world. A human? Perhaps he was close to a town, or maybe this was a hunter in search of game.

"Hey!" Larten called, shouting through a cupped hand to amplify his voice.

But if it was a person, they either didn't hear him or ignored him.

Larten changed direction. It was probably nothing, a leaf or a scrap of cloth, but hope drove him on. If it was a person, he could hand over the baby. Maybe the boy didn't have to die with the vampire. Instead of a cave, he might wind up in a cottage with a fire burning brightly in one corner and a pail of warm milk to drink from.

There was only ice in the place where Larten had glimpsed movement. He stood, peering into the snow-riddled darkness, trying not to breathe. For a long time he saw nothing. But then, as the wind briefly died down, he caught sight of it again, a long way off, something green and yellow. He started to cry out, but lost sight of the object once more as the storm revived.

Larten trailed the phantom for the rest of the night. The longer he chased it, the more convinced he became that it wasn't real. He thought a ghost was leading him to his doom, toying with him cruelly. Or the snow had impaired his vision and the occasional flashes of green and yellow were nothing more than a flare at the back of his eyes. If he'd been alone, he would have abandoned the colors and their mocking promise of hope. But as long as the baby breathed, Larten owed him. If there was even the slimmest of chances that this might prove the saving of the boy, Larten had to seize it.

So he pushed on, through snow, over ice, defying the bitter wind. Cold was setting in again, despite his covering of fur. He could feel himself drawing close to the end. Even vampires had their limits. As plagued as he'd been with sickness recently, it was a miracle he had made it this far. He tried chewing a piece of meat to renew his strength, but it only made him feel sick.

He had bottles of blood, taken from the few sailors he'd spared on the ship, but he was reluctant to drink. Human blood was nectar to a vampire. He could go a long way on a small amount. If he drank now, he'd find the strength to continue, but that would carry him farther than he cared. He didn't want another week of life. So he left the bottles buried deep beneath his shirt and stumbled on.

Shortly after dawn, as he readjusted the fur to protect his face from the weak sunlight, the green and yellow flashes vanished. He had lost track of them many times before, only to catch another flicker out of the corner of his eye a few minutes later, so he waited calmly. But eventually he realized the colors – if they'd existed in the first place – had disappeared for good. He and the baby were alone, stranded and more lost than ever.

Larten sneered at the wind and snow. He should have known better. He had let himself be distracted when all that mattered was finding a cave. There was no hope for the baby in this damned land. All he'd done was waste time and make it more likely that the child would have to rot in the open with him.

"The same old Larten," he muttered. "Always indecisive. But no more."

He straightened and let the rough cloak of blood-stained fur drop to the snowy ground. Enough was enough. He was going to do what he should have done as soon as he got ashore—dig a hole and bury the baby alive. Not a pleasant way for the boy to die, but at least his suffering would be short. It would be hard digging through ice and frozen earth, but his vampire nails were a match for the job. Once the grim deed was done, he could go in search of his own death.

Larten stopped halfway into a crouch. The wind

had dropped for a second and he'd spotted an opening in a rocky ridge to his left. It looked like the mouth of a cave.

For a long moment Larten stared slack-jawed at the ridge. Was this real? If so, perhaps the colors had been too. Maybe the yellow and green flashes had been shades of the baby's parents, leading Larten to this place, so that their son could be laid to rest in a proper tomb. It was unlikely, but Larten had seen and heard of stranger things.

Sighing, he picked up the fur, covered himself and the boy again, and set off towards the hole in the rock. One way or another he was determined to part ways with the baby at the ridge. Death had been cheated long enough. It was time to pay the grim reaper his due.

It wasn't a cave. It was a palace of the dead.

Larten couldn't believe it at first. The opening in the rock was larger than it had looked from afar, but he'd assumed it was no more than an ordinary cave. He entered happily, glad to be out of the bite of the wind, thinking maybe this would be a good place for him to die too. He stood within the entrance awhile, letting his eyes adjust to the darkness.

And then he realized it wasn't that dark. The

world behind him was sparkling beneath the rays of the day's young sun, but the cave ahead was illuminated too. There was a source of light at the other end. Frowning, Larten made sure one of his knives was within easy reach – he felt nervous for some reason – then inched forward, whispering to the baby to keep him quiet.

When the tunnel opened out into a great cavern, Larten forgot about his knife, the baby, and everything else, and just stared around in silent, dumbstruck wonder.

Like many of the halls of Vampire Mountain, this monumental cave had started out as a natural feature, but had been worked on by other hands since nature last applied her touch. Rocks had been removed from the ceiling and panels of crystal inserted in their place. That was why the cave was bright—the light of the sun reflected through the crystals.

Symbols and pictures had been carved into the walls, along with words, row after row of text, encircling the cavern. Larten had never learned to read, so he wasn't sure what language it was, but from the different styles he assumed more than one person had worked on the carvings.

There were dozens of ice sculptures dotted around

the cavern and hanging by ropes from the ceiling. Some of the sculptures were of objects—a chandelier that looked like it was decorated with candles, a drinking fountain, a four-poster bed, several chairs and thrones. Others were of men, or to be more precise, *vampires*. Even if there hadn't been the marks on their fingertips and the scars of warfare on their faces and limbs, Larten would have known. One vampire always recognized another, even if that other was only an icen statue.

The grandest sculpture stood at the center of the cavern. It was a perfect replica of Vampire Mountain, carved out of ice, twenty feet tall. Larten felt a pang of homesickness, which surprised him—after all, he hadn't been forced out of the mountain, but had left of his own accord.

At the foot of the giant sculpture sat a long coffin made of ice. Others were spread around the hall, an almost perfect circle of them, only disturbed in two places by a chasm that Larten would soon explore. But first the main coffin. He didn't want to die before his curiosity had been sated.

The coffin was beautifully decorated with carvings of wolves, bats and bears. Weapons were buried within the ice, a sword, several knives and an ax.

They surrounded the body of a naked vampire, one of the finest warriors the clan had ever produced. As Larten drew abreast of the corpse, he peered through the lid of ice at the face of the vampire inside, preserved as if he'd died only a few nights ago. He noted the missing hand and half a missing jaw, but he didn't need those features to identify the dead General. He'd known as soon as he set foot inside the cavern. Part of him had known when he saw the opening in the ridge from afar.

"*Perta Vin-Grahl*," Larten sighed, and knelt before the final resting place of the vampire who had passed into the realms of myth hundreds of years before.

When the vampaneze broke away from the clan, Perta Vin-Grahl fought harder than anyone to eliminate the traitors. He hated the breakaway group, but loved the vampire clan even more. When the Princes agreed to a truce, Perta couldn't accept their decision. In order not to clash with his leaders and create more problems, he led a group of similarly inclined vampires away into the frozen wilds to perish out of sight and mind.

One of Perta's group returned years later with tales of a tomb like a palace and coffins made of ice.

For centuries nobody knew if the stories were true. Many had searched for Perta Vin-Grahl's final resting place, but none had found it. Until now.

Larten studied the face of the dead General and smiled weakly. It was ironic that such a noble vampire should have been discovered by a disgraceful failure. Destiny had a wicked sense of humor. Seba or Vancha should have had this honor, even Wester. Not pitiful Larten Crepsley.

For a moment Larten considered taking the news back to the clan. Nobody knew what had happened on the ship. If he withheld that information, and only spoke of his incredible find, he would be embraced by the Princes, saluted by the Generals, respected by all. The future would be his.

But Larten hadn't been reared to lie. Seba had taught him, above all else, to be honest. If he returned with his tale, he must tell all. He couldn't accept a life of half-truths. And since he didn't wish to admit his shame to his old master, he decided it would be for the best if he stayed true to his original course.

"My apologies if I disturbed your slumber, General," Larten murmured, then dug out the baby from beneath his makeshift cloak and set him on top of the coffin. The boy gasped from the cold, then laughed and wriggled his legs. Larten smiled and gently touched the baby's cheek. He'd meant to bury the child, but he no longer thought that was essential. This was a place of death, but there was also some form of strange magic in the air. Perhaps the ghosts of the frozen Generals guarded it, or maybe it was some other force, but Larten was certain the baby's corpse wouldn't be disturbed here, even out in the open, atop the coffin of ice.

"Even in death may you be triumphant, young one," he said softly, then left the boy to freeze. It wouldn't take long, and he couldn't think of a better place for the innocent baby to lie than over the preserved remains of the legendary Perta Vin-Grahl.

Leaving the cloak of fur on the floor by the coffin, Larten strode to the edge of the chasm running through the cave. The crack in the ice started at one side and ran all the way across to the other. It was five feet wide at its narrowest, fifteen at its widest. It was a relatively recent fissure—a couple of coffins at opposite sides had fallen into it, and others nearby had been disturbed.

Larten gazed down into the abyss. He couldn't see the bottom. The crack seemed to stretch all the way to the center of the earth. He picked up a stone and dropped it, but there was no sound of it landing.

"So it ends," Larten whispered, wondering how long he would fall, if there was ice at the bottom or fiery magma. Maybe this was a supernatural rip and ghosts would attack him and keep him alive, suspend and torment him. In this mysterious, eerie cave he could believe just about anything.

Larten was eager to leap, but first he made himself remember his master, Seba Nile, and praised his name. He thought about Wester too, the vampire who had been like his brother. The Princes, Vancha, Malora, Evanna. He considered them one by one and said a few words for each, apologizing to those who might be hurt by his suicide. No vampire could be proud of taking his own life, but if you had to, there was a right way and a wrong way to go about it. This would be Larten's final act and he didn't want to pass poorly from this world.

When he had said his farewells, Larten stared once again into the abyss and smiled. He was glad it was over. Sorry that things had come to this, but at least he need suffer no more. If he was reborn and given a second chance, as some believed, he would try to do better next time around. In this life he had struggled from the start and it was maybe for the best that he was done with it.

Larten wanted to roar the death cry of the clan – "Even in death may I be triumphant!" – but there could be no triumph for him in suicide. Keeping his lips tight, he leaned forward and let himself fall.

As he toppled over the edge, his eyes widened. Imminent death has a way of focusing the senses, and in that moment Larten knew he was a fool. Yes, he had strayed, hit rock bottom, shamed himself and disappointed those who had tried to help him over the years. But life had been given to him by a higher force and he had no right to surrender his grip on it so cheaply. He should have fought on and done all that he could to redeem himself. This was selfish and wasteful. *Cowardly*. Nobody should voluntarily give up on life. If it was your time to die, death would calmly claim you. Otherwise it was your duty to press on and live.

Larten cried out with dismay and flapped his arms wildly to regain his balance. But it was too late. His weight had carried him clear of the ledge and he was falling. There could be no going back. Gravity had hold and all that lay ahead of him now was the fall, the crash and . . .

24

A hand grabbed the back of his shirt and Larten came to a stunned halt. Then, as his life hung in the balance and he blinked with confusion and dread, someone chuckled and said, "Well, well, what have we here?"

Chapter Three

Larten tried to turn around to see who had hold of him. As he did, his shirt ripped and he lurched forward again.

"Careful," the stranger tutted, grabbing another handful of shirt. "These stitches were not meant to take such a strain. If you don't keep *very* still, they'll snap and that will be the end of you."

Larten gulped and stared at the drop beneath him. He had never felt so desperate to live. Or so helpless. "Who are you?" he gasped.

"The eye of the storm," the man answered cryptically. "The heart of the sun. The shadow in your soul." He paused solemnly, then teasingly added, "But you can call me Desmond."

Larten had thought he could never feel any colder than when he'd been trudging through the purgatorial snow, but when he realized who had hold of him, a chill spread from the pit of his stomach that was even icier than the coffin of Perta Vin-Grahl. "*Mr. Tiny!*" Larten cried.

There was an approving grunt. "My reputation has preceded me. That is how it should be. Now tell me, Master Crepsley, do you want to live or shall I let you fall?"

Larten's throat tightened. Mr. Tiny waited a few seconds, then shook him playfully. "It's all the same to me, dear boy. This doesn't have to be a reprieve. I can release you if you wish. Just say the word and..."

Larten felt the small man's fingers loosening. "No!" he screamed.

"I didn't think so," Mr. Tiny laughed and suddenly Larten was flying through the air. But not the air of the chasm—Mr. Tiny had thrown him across the room and he landed in an untidy heap near the base of Perta Vin-Grahl's coffin, on top of which the baby was still wriggling and gurgling.

Larten sat up, panting heavily, and watched the infamous meddler come towards him with a curious waddle. The tiny man had white hair, rosy cheeks and a thick pair of spectacles. He was dressed in a bright yellow suit and a green pair of boots. Larten recalled the flashes of color that he had followed to this cave. "You led me here," he muttered.

"Do you think so?" Mr. Tiny smiled.

"I saw green and yellow when I was in the snow."

Mr. Tiny seemed to consider that. "It might have been me," he conceded. "Or it might have been coincidence." He beamed and there was nothing remotely warm in his smile. "Or it could have been *destiny*."

Mr. Tiny stopped close to Larten and gazed around the cavern. There was a large, heart-shaped watch pinned to his breast pocket. Larten had heard many vampires comment on that watch and wonder at its true purpose. Mr. Tiny was older than any of the clan. According to the legends, he had been on this planet before the rise of vampire or man, maybe before life itself began. Nobody knew how powerful he was, or what his exact designs might be, but his love of chaos and suffering had been well documented over the millennia.

"I made a nice job of it, didn't I?" Mr. Tiny said,

nodding at the roof. "You'd never believe how difficult it was to fit those crystals."

Larten frowned. "*You* created this?"

"Just the roof," Mr. Tiny said modestly. "Perta and his cronies did the rest. I added the crystals to cast more of a shine on things. You don't have to worry," he added. "The crystals filter the rays of the sun. This light can't do you any harm."

Larten hadn't been thinking about the beams, but now that his attention was drawn to it, he realized he felt none of the pain that he did in normal sunlight.

"I like this place," Mr. Tiny said. "It's atmospheric. I often come here when I'm in a reflective mood and want to get away from the hustle and bustle of the modern world. Even the mightiest of us need our *time-outs*, as humans will refer to it in another few decades or so."

Larten failed to pick up on Mr. Tiny's reference to the future. He was more concerned with why the diminutive man of magic had led him here...why his life had been spared...and what Desmond Tiny was planning for him next.

"Why did you save me?" Larten asked.

Mr. Tiny sniffed. "You didn't want to die. Most

mortals don't, even if they find themselves in as desolate and soul-destroying a spot as you. Almost all of those who take their own lives wish at the last moment that they hadn't. They see at the end how much they've given up, how precious life is, even when it's treated them like dirt and crushed their dreams. Many think they've passed beyond hope, but they never really have, not until they pass beyond life itself. Alas, that knowledge comes too late for most would-be suicides and they die with regret. Very few are offered the chance that you have been handed."

"And I appreciate it greatly," Larten said truthfully. "But why save *me*? Out of all who teeter on the edge, why pull *me* back?"

Mr. Tiny shrugged. "It was your destiny."

Larten shook his head. "My destiny was to fall. You changed it."

"Did I?" Mr. Tiny's eyes sparkled. "Maybe it was *my* destiny to save you. In that case *this* was your true destiny, not death." Mr. Tiny laughed at Larten's confused expression. "Fate might seem like a complex puzzle, but it's simple at its core. Near misses and might-have-beens are nothing more than shadows of destiny. Each man has only one true path in life. You thought that yours ended here. You were wrong."

Mr. Tiny approached the baby and tickled his stomach. As the boy giggled, Mr. Tiny asked, "Does he have a name?"

"No," Larten said.

"Every mortal should have a name," Mr. Tiny murmured. "It separates you from the beasts of the wild. How about we call him... *Gavner Purl*?"

Larten blinked dumbly. "As good a name as any, I suppose."

"Then Gavner Purl it is." Mr. Tiny smiled and licked his lips. "Now that we've named him, how about we carve him up and share him between us? Little Gavner looks tasty."

"Leave him alone," Larten snapped, standing quickly and snatching the boy from the drooling man in the yellow suit.

"Be careful," Mr. Tiny said coldly. "I don't take kindly to orders. If I want the child, I'll take him." He smiled again. "But I don't. You can have the mewling, bony thing. I already ate today." Mr. Tiny nodded politely at Larten and turned towards the exit.

"Wait!" Larten called him back. "You cannot simply walk out on us. You never answered my question about why you saved me."

Mr. Tiny shrugged. "And I have no intention of

doing so. I helped you because it was my wish. That's all you need to know."

"And now you are just going to leave me?" Larten asked.

"Yes," Mr. Tiny said. "I've done all that I care to do for you. You're on your own from this point on."

"What if I jump into the chasm again?"

"You won't," Mr. Tiny said confidently.

"But how will we get out of here?" Larten roared as Mr. Tiny headed for the tunnel. "The baby cannot endure the cold much longer. I do not know where we are. We have nothing to eat. How will we survive and get back to civilization?"

"You'll find a way, I'm sure," Mr. Tiny answered without looking around. And then he was gone, leaving an astonished Larten and a hungry Gavner Purl alone with the dead in the palace of coffins and ice.

Part Two

"then there will come a time
of reckoning"

Chapter Four

As the engine roared and the aircraft picked up speed and bounced over the grass, Larten glanced around and thought, *This is never going to fly!* The wings looked like six boxes, three on either side, a mix of bamboo and silk, joined by something that Alberto had called aluminum. How could a contraption like this ever leave the ground?

"Go on, Vur!" Alicia cried, shaking her fist in the light of the almost-full moon. "You can do it!"

Alberto stood next to her, doubled over with laughter. He'd told Larten not to try – no amateur could fly his *14-bis*, his beloved *bird of prey* – but Alicia had dared him and Larten never backed away from a dare.

"By the black blood of Harnon Oan!" Larten growled, then pulled on the lever that was meant to control the craft. To his astonishment – as well as Alicia's and Alberto's – the aircraft lifted a few feet. He flew for all of five seconds before the wheels hit the ground. He thought that would be the end of it, but the aircraft continued to power ahead, and when he tried the lever again he rose maybe nine feet in the air and flew for eighty or ninety feet before crashing back to earth.

One of the wings dipped and tipped towards the ground. Moments later the aircraft screeched to an abrupt halt and Larten was thrown forward to roll across the grass until he came to a painful stop.

"Vur!" Alicia yelled, racing after him. "Are you all right? Have you broken any bones, my darling?"

"I am intact," Larten muttered, standing and wincing.

When Alicia saw that he hadn't been seriously injured, she threw herself into his arms and knocked him down again. Larten was laughing by the time Alberto caught up with him, mock-wrestling with the beautiful Alicia.

"That was superb!" Alberto applauded. "It must have been a hundred feet at least."

"I think slightly less," Larten said.

"Even so...*magnifique*! I've managed no more than two hundred feet myself and I'm an expert."

"You do not need to be an expert to fly one of these," Larten sniffed. "Just insane."

"Didn't you enjoy it, darling?" Alicia asked.

"No," he grunted. "Monsieur Santos-Dumont and the Wright Brothers can wage their war for the air without me. I have experienced all the *joys* of flight I ever intend to. It is a crazy form of transport, Alberto. If you heed my advice, you will get out of this business immediately. There is no future in aircrafts."

With that, the smiling vampire turned his back on the shuddering machine and never stepped aboard an aeroplane again.

Paris in 1906 was a chic, vibrant, multilayered wonder. The Eiffel Tower, still standing seventeen years after it had been erected as a temporary exhibit for the Universal Exposition, was the tallest building in the world. The métro had opened six years ago, providing Parisians with a fascinating ride deep beneath the streets. The city was flooded with artists, many hoping to improve on the advances made some years earlier by the Impressionists. It had the most acclaimed museums, the finest restaurants, the rowdiest night-life. From the respectability of the Louvre to the seed-iness of the Moulin Rouge, Paris had something for everyone.

For Larten Crepsley, above all else it had Alicia Dunyck, a woman with whom he'd fallen in love.

They had met for the first time four years earlier, when Larten turned up in Paris at random. He had been going by the name of Vur Horston, which was how Alicia still knew him. After what he had done on the ship to Greenland, he wanted to try to forget about Larten Crepsley, at least for a while, possibly forever.

Gavner brought the pair of them together. The baby had survived the trek back from the icy wastes and grown into a sturdy little boy. It would have been easy for Larten to rear him as his son, but he didn't feel that he had the right. He had never lost sight of the fact that he had killed the boy's parents. He believed it would be hypocrisy of the highest order if he took their place and let the boy love him as a father.

Although Larten fed and cared for Gavner on their way back, he was stern with the boy and refused to treat him with love. He believed a night would come when he and the adult Gavner Purl must address the nature of his foul crime. He didn't want any sort of emotional attachment to confuse the orphan when that night came.

Larten tried to offload the boy a number of times, but nobody seemed to want him. He could have abandoned Gavner and left him to the workings of fate, but he needed to be sure that the boy would have a chance to prosper. So he kept Gavner by his side longer than he would have liked, crossing the world with no real plan, waiting for the right set of parents to accept the growing child.

In Paris he finally found a home for the boy. He had made money gambling, and attracted a wealthy circle of fair-weather friends. He had no interest in these vain, frivolous people except to find parents for Gavner. Wealth wasn't important to Larten, but the rich had a much easier time in life than the poor, so he thought he might as well settle the boy with a prosperous couple.

He met Alicia by chance. She was the cousin of one of the men he gambled with. She came one night to experience a little of her cousin's sordid world. Alicia stood out among the others in the saloon. She didn't consider herself superior to the women of low class or the men of dark vices, or look upon them with disdain. But there was a sadness in her expression as she watched the lost creatures chase their petty pleasures. Larten, who knew much about sadness, was moved by it and made an excuse to talk with her and meet her again in a place more fitting than a den of wine, women and cards.

Alicia was suspicious of the pale, scarred, orange-haired man of mystery. There were many rumors about the strange Vur Horston, that he'd made his money from the illegal slave trade, that he was a highly paid assassin, that he avoided the sun because he had signed a contract with the devil and would burst into flame if exposed to the pure light of the day world.

"Nothing so dramatic," Larten laughed when Alicia put this accusation to him. "I have a severe skin condition, that is all."

She was wary of the stranger and didn't encourage further visits, but Larten was persistent, popping up wherever she went, bending her ear, discussing art and dancing with her. (He had no great love of either, but made an effort to impress.) He realized that lavish presents wouldn't impress her, so instead he scoured the markets for quirky, beautiful flowers or charming, cracked ornaments, which were worthless but came with an interesting story.

As she slowly warmed to him, Larten introduced her to Gavner, who was a sullen, quiet boy. Gavner knew Larten preferred silence and a sense of distance, so he was more withdrawn than most children. Like all young boys, he craved love, but having received none from the man who refused to act as his father, he hoped to earn Larten's approval by behaving as coldly as the adult did.

Larten didn't tell Alicia that he was hoping to give away the boy. Instead he told her that Gavner was the son of an old friend and that he'd vowed to look after the orphan when his parents died. He let her think it was his intention to bring up Gavner on his own.

"Why are you so hard on him?" Alicia asked not long after she got to know the child. "You're kind and gentle with me. Why not with Gavner?"

"I raise him the way I was raised," Larten answered stiffly. "Discipline is good for a growing boy."

"But you push him away every time he tries to get close to you," she said.

Larten grunted sourly, but inside he was smiling. As he had hoped, Alicia made even more of an effort with Gavner, encouraging him to smile, laugh, play and enjoy the world. A bond grew between them, and although Alicia was young and free, with hopes of having children of her own one day, she didn't hesitate when Larten asked if she wished to take the boy and rear him as her son.

That should have been the end of the matter. Larten had finally rid himself of his charge and was free to search for a place in the wide, lonely world. But he had grown fond of Alicia, so he made one excuse after another to stay. Weeks became months, and months became years. He still occasionally spoke of leaving, but it had been a long time since he'd truly meant it. He had found unexpected peace in Paris, and while he refused to admit it, deep down he hoped to stay with Alicia to the end of her relatively short, normal life.

They returned home after Larten's adventure in the aircraft, still laughing. Alberto Santos-Dumont was a good friend of Alicia's. She couldn't understand his obsession with building the first *proper* aircraft ("The Wrights use catapults to launch their clumsy contraptions! How can that be a real aircraft?" he would protest whenever the American pioneers were mentioned), but she enjoyed watching the machines that he built, especially when they got off the ground. Larten didn't normally come with her when she visited Alberto – he preferred night pursuits to those of the day – but he was fascinated by her reports. When he'd casually declared that any fool could fly the simple aircraft, she put the challenge to Alberto and convinced him to let Larten try the *14-bis* one bright, moonlit night.

"You could be an aircraft operator," Alicia joked as they let themselves in. "Alberto says there will be large aircraft soon, with seats for passengers. You could get a job flying people from one town to another."

"Alberto lives in a fantasy world," Larten snorted. "Aircraft are a novelty. They will never replace trains or boats. Only a fool would think otherwise."

"I don't know," Alicia sang, tweaking his nose, then went to check on Gavner. He was fast asleep and snoring heavily. She'd never known anyone who snored as loudly as Gavner Purl.

Larten was staring out the window when she returned. He was thinking about Malora and the people on the ship, as he often did in quiet moments like this. No matter how much happiness he found with Alicia, the sorrows of the past were never far from his thoughts.

Alicia studied him, gazing at his troubled reflection in the glass, wishing she could do something to rid him of his grief. There was much about his life that was a secret. She knew he'd had an unhappy past, that he was hiding a lot from her. But that didn't matter. She loved him and was sure he'd reveal the full truth to her in time. And no matter how disturbing it was, she would still love him and do what she could to help him deal with it.

After all, she thought as she slid forward and embraced Larten, bringing a smile to his thin lips, *it can't be that bad. No matter what life has thrown at him, regardless of what he did in his youth, he is a good man at heart. His dark deeds are probably nowhere near as grisly as he believes. And if they are? Well, I'll forgive him. We all make mistakes. That's simply the nature of what we are. I'll confess mine and accept his. He has set his standards high, and that is admirable, but he should not be so hard on himself. After all, I will tell him, at the end of the day, like the rest of us, he's only human....*

Chapter Five

Larten was a night creature, but he made adjustments to his routines to account for Alicia and, to a lesser extent, Gavner. Although he avoided mornings and the searing light of the midday world, he normally rose in the early afternoon to spend some of the day with Alicia and the boy. He would listen to Gavner reading – something he'd never learned to do himself – and gruffly tell the child that he was doing a good job if he made no obvious mistakes. The three of them would go out for walks or to the shops, Larten shielded from the sun by an umbrella, hat and gloves, wearing dark glasses to protect his eyes.

Alicia thought he was exaggerating about his condition until one day he sat by a window for half an hour with his arms and face exposed. When she saw the way his skin reddened, she realized he was telling the truth. From that day on she was even more conscious of the sun than he was.

As they strolled through a park one cloudy evening, Gavner running ahead of them trying to catch a bird, Alicia squeezed Larten's arm and pecked his scarred cheek beneath the covering of the umbrella.

"What was that for?" he asked.

"Nothing. I'm just happy." She squeezed his arm again. "This is a good life, isn't it, Vur?"

"Aye," he said, feeling the little stab of guilt he always did when she called him by his false name. He knew he should tell her the truth about himself, but he hoped that if he denied the reality of Larten Crepsley long enough, the man he'd once been might cease to exist entirely.

"Gavner is happy too," she murmured. Larten stiffened, as she'd guessed he would, and she tutted loudly. "You have to stop that," she snapped.

"Stop what?" Larten frowned.

"Gavner is our child," she said. It was an old argument, one she had with him a couple of times a month. "You should start treating him like your son. He needs a father, and you're all he has. Unless you'd rather I look for another man to take me on walks through the park..." She grinned cheekily at him.

"You might be better off with another man," Larten said gloomily, and Alicia pinched him.

"You'll say that once too often one day," she growled.

Larten forced a smile, but he was troubled. Alicia was right. Gavner *did* need a father. He had grown into a bright, healthy, good-natured boy, blooming under the care of his foster mother. But he often stared at Larten longingly. He didn't know why the tall man with the scar brushed him aside whenever he tried to get close. He thought there must be something wrong with him, that he had in some way offended the adult. Although he was happy and lively around Alicia, Gavner pulled back into himself when he was with other children. He thought they might reject him if he tried to be friendly with them, as his guardian had.

He deserves better, Larten thought sadly. *He deserves a father. But I can never be that for him. I killed his true parents. I must never let him love me. Never.*

He should leave. He was a thorn in Gavner's side, a shadow hanging over the boy. If he left, Alicia would find another man to marry her, as Larten had so far failed to do, despite her many hints that she would accept his proposal if he asked. That man could be a real father to Gavner and the boy would profit from their relationship.

But that would mean abandoning Alicia. The small woman with the red hair and green eyes had brought happiness into Larten's life, a type he'd never suspected he might be capable of experiencing. He couldn't walk away from that. With her, he could nearly forget about Malora, the killings, the dark abyss into which he had almost literally fallen. If he cut her out of his life, he feared what might happen to him next.

"Vur?" Alicia asked quietly, breaking his gloomy reverie.

For a moment he thought she was calling to the real Vur Horston and he looked around eagerly for a thin, unwell boy he hadn't seen in close to a hundred years. But when he only found the chubby Gavner Purl – still chasing the bird – he realized she was speaking to him. "Yes?" he replied.

"A centime for your thoughts," Alicia said.

Larten smiled thinly. "They are not worth that much."

Then he held her close and strolled after the running, laughing boy, afraid that he'd lose her – and himself – forever if he let her go.

A few nights after their walk in the park, Alicia dragged Larten along to an art exhibition. Among the works on display were some new paintings by a young Spanish artist called Pablo Picasso. Larten liked most of the art, but he wasn't too keen on the crowd.

Larten was uncomfortable in large gatherings. When it was just him and Alicia, he could forget that he was different. In other company he became self-conscious. He kept expecting someone to recognize him for what he truly was and scream *"Vampire!"* The book by that dratted Bram Stoker had come out some years before and everyone knew the word now. There was no point claiming innocence and saying he wasn't like the fictional Dracula. Larten knew how mobs worked. If his true identity was ever revealed, he would have no choice but to flee.

Larten had been uneasy since they arrived at the exhibition. As they wandered, stopping to chat with friends of Alicia's, that feeling intensified. He felt certain that he was being watched. Some people might have dismissed such a hunch, but Larten knew better than to doubt his instincts.

The vampire smiled freely and pretended to listen to the conversation flowing around him. He didn't want to let the person watching him know that he was aware of their scrutiny. But all the time he was slyly sweeping the rooms with his gaze, searching for the one who had pinpointed him.

Finally he singled out his potential enemy. It was a tall, fat man. He was twice the size of anybody else and Larten was surprised not to have noticed him before. The man's face was virtually hidden behind layers of blubber. He had long, curled hair and a majestic, drooping, waxed mustache. He was finely dressed, his fingers – Larten noted without surprise that each one had a small scar at the tip – glittered with rings, and he sported a diamond-studded monocle. But there was something vulgar about him, and it wasn't just the four scantily clad women who encircled him and tittered at his every joke.

The fat man saw that he had been spotted. With a sharp word and a curt snap of his hand he dismissed the women. They drifted away to talk with some of the other men – they had plenty of admirers – though Larten was sure they'd return once their master clicked his scar-tipped fingers. They were the type of women he had seen much of in his younger days as a vampire Cub.

The fat man inclined his head and stepped out onto a balcony, inviting Larten to follow. "Excuse me a moment," he murmured to Alicia. "I wish to take some air."

"Don't be long," she said.

"Of course not," he promised, but he wasn't sure if he could keep this particular vow. He didn't know what the fat man wanted, but he was sure of one thing—the stranger was a vampire. And that spelled bad news whatever way he looked at it.

The obese vampire was snorting a pinch of snuff when Larten joined him on the balcony. He offered some, but Larten shook his head.

"You never did like snuff, did you?" the man purred, putting it away.

"You know me, sir?" Larten frowned, studying the stranger again, trying to place him. There was something familiar about the voice, but not the man's face. Had they met in Vampire Mountain?

"I know you well, Vur Horston," the man smirked.

"I also knew you when you went by your real name. And I knew you by another name too." His eyes twinkled and Larten realized that whoever this was, the man meant him no harm.

"What name might that have been?" Larten asked, relaxing slightly.

"It was one I gave you myself," the vampire said, then smiled nervously as he removed his monocle and brushed his hair back, revealing his face in full. "I called you Quicksilver."

The mention of his old nickname astonished Larten, but as the man formed the word, something about the movement of his lips triggered a memory that was even more astonishing. Leaning close, eyes widening with shock, Larten seized the man's shoulders and croaked with disbelief, *"Tanish Eul?"*

Chapter Six

Larten and Tanish sat in plush leather chairs in the study of Tanish's house, sipping wine from France's finest vineyards. Larten preferred ale to wine, but Tanish was proud of his collection and forced a glass on his guest.

Larten had known Tanish when they were Cubs, young vampires with a taste for war and the seedier human pleasures. They'd drunk, gambled and womanized their way across much of the world. He had counted Tanish as a close friend, one who got him into much trouble, but who was always fun company. Then Tanish refused the challenge of a vampaneze and was shamed in front of his peers. He departed in disgrace, never again to take his place in the clan. Larten thought that was the last he would see of the dashing, finely groomed vampire. Over the years he had occasionally wondered what might have happened to Tanish, but only idly, never expecting an answer.

Now here was the exile, bloated beyond recognition, wealthy and dressed in the most expensive clothes that Paris could offer, with a coterie of pretty young women and faithful servants.

"I knew you as soon as I saw you," Tanish said for the umpteenth time. "The scar's new, but otherwise you look the same. Not me! I've fattened out, haven't I, Quicksilver?"

"You have," Larten smiled. "But please, call me Vur."

"Afraid I might ruin your cover?" Tanish smirked.

"Aye," Larten admitted. He'd sent Alicia home, only telling her that he had met an old friend with whom he had much to discuss. Alicia wanted to meet Tanish Eul, but Larten had asked for some time alone with him.

"There's no need to fear my tongue," Tanish said. "Discretion is vital to me too. We both have secrets we wish to keep safe. I'll say nothing of your past, *Vur Horston*."

Larten thanked Tanish, then remarked on how well he seemed to be doing.

"Not bad," Tanish sniffed, waving a hand at the beautifully decorated walls, the statues and paintings, the giant chandelier. The room was as big as the apartment where Larten and Alicia lived, and it was only one of many in the mansion, which was situated in the most fashionable part of Paris. "Of course this is just my town house. My place in the country is grander. I like an intimate setting when I come to the city."

"It must have cost a fortune," Larten noted. "You cannot have made such profits from gambling, surely."

"Actually I did," Tanish said. "But from the other side of the table. I run several casinos. There's more to be made hosting gamblers than playing with them. Most of my profits come from drink and my pretty things, though I get a cut of all the table action too."

Larten frowned. "What are your *pretty things*?"

"Women," Tanish laughed. "We never had problems attracting young maids, did we? But others aren't as lucky with the ladies as we were. For a price I supply the wealthier men of Paris with an introduction to companions who warmly welcome their attention."

"Ah," Larten sighed.

"You disapprove?" Tanish asked quietly.

"No," Larten said. "I am merely surprised. I thought you might have gone into legitimate business. Having traveled so widely, I assumed import and export would have been more your line."

"I rarely travel these days," Tanish said. "No more than I have to. The world's the same no matter where you go. Better to find a spot you can call home, then set down roots. I realized that long ago and I think you've come to see it too. That lady you were with tonight didn't look as if she was going anywhere soon, and you plan to stay by her side a while, aye?"

"As long as she will have me," Larten murmured.

"The years have been hard for you," Tanish said seriously. "I see it in your eyes. Life in the clan wasn't all that you imagined, eh, old friend?"

"No," Larten said softly and that was all he had to say about it.

"Leaving that dark, insular world was the best thing I ever did," Tanish sniffed. "The clan's fine for the likes of Vancha March and those who think life is a trial that we should endure. But it's not fitting for men of culture and refinement. You and I were meant for nobler things. The pleasures of the human world are best appreciated by those who have superseded humanity."

There was a bell by Tanish's chair. He picked it up and shook it twice. A man entered the room. Larten thought he was a servant, but at a click of Tanish's fingers the man knelt by the side of the vampire's chair. Tanish put a nail to the man's neck and made a small incision. Leaning forward, wheezing as the layers of fat tightened around his stomach, he stuck out his tongue and lapped at the blood like a cat. When he was done, he spat on the man's neck and rubbed in the spit to stop the flow of blood.

"Are you thirsty?" Tanish asked, nudging the man towards Larten.

"No," Larten said.

"You're sure I can't tempt you?"

"I drank earlier," Larten lied.

Tanish dismissed the man and smiled in an ugly way as the pitiful figure left the room, head bowed, silent as a ghost. "He wants to become a vampire," Tanish sneered. "He thinks we live forever and are impervious to harm. I have others like him. I'll never blood them – I know how scrupulous the Generals are, curse their eyes – but it amuses me to watch them squirm in the hope of joining our allegedly illustrious ranks."

"Is it wise to let them know what you are?" Larten asked. "Especially given the current climate."

"The...? Oh, you mean that *Dracula* book." Tanish waved it away. "They'll do as I say. I don't keep them against their will. They think vampires are like gods. If one of them ever threatens to betray me... well, any god worth his salt is due a sacrifice every now and then, isn't he?"

Tanish chortled at Larten's expression. "I'm joking! I'd never kill those who serve me. I'm lazy, fat and foolish. I spend more than I should and chase women who only want me for my money. I have many vices, some that might shock even a hardened man of the world like you. But I'm not a killer." His face softened. "You should know that better than any. You saw what happened when I was challenged. I'm a coward, aye, but not so craven that I'd kill weak humans to make myself feel powerful. I hope you know me well enough not to think so ill of me."

"Of course," Larten said, leaning across to pat the fat man's pudgy knee. "Now tell me more about the past. I would like to know what you did when you left the clan, how you built your empire of sin."

Tanish smiled at that – he liked the barbed compliment – and launched into a detailed history of his adventures since turning his back on the vampire world. It was a simple story of a man with more power and skill than humans, and how he had abused his talents, but Tanish told it skillfully, making Larten laugh on many occasions.

But there was a sad tinge to Tanish's tales, and although he put a bright spin on things, Larten knew the exiled vampire wasn't truly happy. He had found no more comfort beyond the reach of the clan than Larten had. As rich and surrounded by cronies and pretty women as he was, Tanish's life was a sham of an existence. And Larten wondered, as he listened to his old friend speak, if this was the sort of wasted, miserable future he himself had to look forward to.

Chapter Seven

There was a knock at the front door. Gavner ran to answer it. When he saw the fat, beaming man on the doorstep, he squealed with excitement and threw himself into the visitor's arms. "Uncle Tanish!" he yelled happily.

"Careful, young cur," Tanish growled. "You'll knock me over if you leap at me like a goat!" But he couldn't hide a smile, even beneath the cover of his drooping mustache. He ruffled Gavner's hair, then passed a box of sweets to the boy. He often brought gifts when he visited. Gavner never asked for any, and would have been equally delighted to see his *uncle* if he'd come empty-handed, but Tanish liked to "spread the joy" everywhere he went.

"Are the happy couple home?" Tanish asked.

"Yes," Gavner said, opening the box and peering inside. "They're in the dining room, posing for the portrait."

"Not finished yet?" Tanish gasped theatrically. "That painter must be the slowest in Paris."

"Alicia doesn't mind," Gavner said confidentially, "but Vur's furious! He sits and glowers like those Indian chiefs in the stories you told me." Gavner crossed his arms and frowned fiercely.

Tanish chortled. "Perhaps I'll bribe the painter to work even slower," he said, and the pair almost collapsed with giggles.

"Wait," Gavner said when Tanish recovered and started for the dining room. "I built a model of the Eiffel Tower that I want to show you."

Tanish went with the boy to his room, where he spent several minutes admiring Gavner's crude re-creation of the famous tower and complimenting the talentless but proud child. "You'll be an architect one day," Tanish said with as straight a face as any he'd ever pulled when playing poker.

When Tanish finally made it out of Gavner's bedroom, he saw that Larten did indeed look the spitting image of an Indian chief and he had to hide his smirk behind a large silk handkerchief. "Many greetings to the master and mistress of the house," he said, sweeping as low as a man his size could. "I hope I have not come at an inopportune time."

"Your timing could not be better," Larten snapped and peeled away from Alicia. The artist had posed them with Larten bending over his loved one. That had been fine to begin with, but this was the eleventh (or was it the twelfth?) sitting and his back had almost seized up.

"Monsieur!" the artist protested. "Another half an hour, please."

"No!" Larten roared. "I have had enough preening for tonight. Go, sir, and take your damn—"

"Vur," Alicia tutted.

Larten scowled and tossed several coins to the indignant artist, who retorted stiffly, "Take care, monsieur. I work as a favor to my clients, not for money. If you continue to treat me this way, I will tear the portrait to shreds and never return." It was a fine speech, but he ruined it when he scrabbled to pick up all the coins from the floor.

The artist was an old enemy of Larten's. Alicia

had originally asked Larten to pose for a drawing with her back in 1903, not long after they had first become a couple. He had only been able to endure a handful of sessions before banishing the artist forever (or so he had assumed).

As the prickly artist departed in a huff, Tanish studied the half-finished canvas. "He has a good eye. Very lifelike. Almost as clear as a photograph."

Tanish exchanged a look with Larten and they both chuckled. Photography was all the rage but neither vampire would ever be captured on film. For some reason no camera could photograph them—they appeared as messy blotches whenever a photo of one of them was developed. That was the only reason Larten had initially agreed to sit for a portrait.

As for why he had relented and invited the artist back to torment him again...Well, in a moment of what he now considered madness, Larten had proposed marriage. A delighted Alicia had swiftly accepted, but insisted they mark their engagement by having the artist finish the portrait that she had been so looking forward to three years earlier. Like all men who had willingly thrown themselves into the marriage trap, Larten had no choice but to agree to the wishes of his beloved.

"The date is wrong," Tanish noted, tapping the large 1903 in the lower right corner of the canvas.

"He will not change it," Larten growled. "That was when he started the painting, and he insists on sticking with the date. I think he has kept it there to remind me of how I insulted him first time around. That will infuriate me whenever I look at the dratted thing. I might paint over it once it is done."

"Don't you dare!" Alicia snapped. "If you even look at the painting in a sour way, there'll be trouble. Understand?"

"Yes, dear," Larten mumbled with uncharacteristic meekness.

"Any advances with the wedding plans?" Tanish asked. It had been three months since Larten took everyone by surprise and asked Alicia to marry him. He still seemed to be in shock, as he went white and trembled whenever actual dates and logistics were mentioned.

"We've settled on a church," Alicia said, then narrowed her eyes. "Haven't we, my darling?"

"Yes, dear," Larten said again, but sulkily this time.

"And it will be sometime next year, correct?" Alicia pressed.

"Aye," Larten sighed.

"Excellent," Tanish applauded. "I'll keep my diary free for the entire year, just to be safe. If I may, I'd recommend June. Brides look so ravishing in the summer."

"Uncle Tanish," Gavner roared, running into the room, cutting Larten short before he could tell Tanish what he thought of his suggestion. "A lift! You forgot to give me a lift."

"Gavner," Alicia sighed. "Where are your manners? That's no way to address Monsieur Eul. You must ask when you want something, not demand."

"Nonsense," Tanish snorted, winking at the boy. "If you want to get anywhere in this world, you have to be forthright. Come, Gavner of the Purls, and let your uncle Tanish lift you to the skies."

Ignoring Alicia's disapproving scowl, Gavner ran to Tanish and stuck up his hands. The fat vampire crouched and Gavner took hold of his honorary uncle's long mustache, grabbing one end in either fist. When he had a firm hold, Tanish twitched his whiskers like a cat, then stood swiftly. Gavner rose into the air with him, dangling from the mustache and wriggling his legs. Larten was reminded of how the

boy had wriggled atop the icy tomb of Perta Vin-
Grahl when he was a baby, and the memory made
him wince.

Tanish made pained, yelping noises and shook his
head wildly, but Gavner knew that he was only playing. Yelling with delight, he swung from the hairy
suspenders and held on as long as he could. When he
finally fell, Tanish pretended to kick him away and
he ran from the room laughing.

"One night he'll rip that mustache out from its
roots," Alicia said warningly.

"That might be for the best," Tanish said. "I think
my glorious whiskers might be going out of fashion."

"Not at all," Larten said, and waited for Tanish's
surprised smile before adding sadistically, "they went
out of fashion twenty years ago."

Alicia laughed, kissed Tanish's cheeks, then went
to fetch wine for their visitor and ale for the man who
would shortly (Next year! He had promised!) be her
husband. Tanish was a regular guest at their apartment. He came two or three times a week, and they
sometimes went to visit him, although Alicia preferred it when he came to them. As much as she loved
Tanish, especially for the way he delighted Gavner,

he was a strange man who surrounded himself with people of low quality and dubious morals. She didn't like exposing Gavner to such dark, seedy facets of the world.

"How goes your life, my scarred, orange-haired freak of a friend?" Tanish asked, settling down on the sofa.

"Much the same as when I saw you last night," Larten smiled.

"Last night?" Tanish frowned. "I don't remember...."

"I came to one of your casinos at your invitation. You had been drinking heavily. You welcomed me warmly, but I did not see much of you after that, and only then through layers of thinly veiled dancers."

"I recall the dancers," Tanish said dreamily, then grinned sheepishly. "I would apologize, Larten, but you know I meant no offense. One of my horses won earlier in the day and I got carried away."

"I thought you were not going to the races yesterday."

"I didn't plan to, but then clouds blew in and I decided it was as good a day as any to venture forth."

Tanish didn't avoid sunlight as scrupulously as

Larten. He had hidden his fear of the day world more cunningly than his friend. While his business gave him the excuse of mainly coming out at night, he made an effort to be seen from time to time when the sun was up, to sidestep the sort of rumors that Larten had attracted. Whenever he went out, he wore hats and gloves, and usually had a troop of his pretty things around him. He always held umbrellas for his female friends, making a joke of it, claiming they were too delicate to support the heavy devices themselves. In fact he slyly sought the shade of the umbrellas more than they did, but nobody had ever noticed.

"I probably wanted to ask if you'd thought about my offer," Tanish said.

"I guessed that was the case," Larten replied.

"And have you?"

Larten shrugged. Tanish had often invited him to get involved with his various businesses, saying they would make great partners. Larten had laughed off his advances to begin with, but Tanish had been more persistent recently, putting real deals before his friend, tempting him with offers of wealth and influence. Larten didn't crave such things for himself, but it would be nice to treat Alicia to the finer fancies of the world, and Gavner would have to be educated. Larten had little love of human luxuries, but he had others to consider now. It would be wrong to propose to Alicia and then carry on as if he were a carefree bachelor.

"I make good money already," Larten said slowly.

"Aye," Tanish huffed. "Stealing when you break in and feed, and picking up a few francs at the gambling tables every now and then. That's no way to make a living. I can give you a real job, honest money and fine opportunities."

"*Honest?*" Larten said with an arch look.

"Well, it's honest in my eyes," Tanish said lightly. "Come, Vur, you have responsibilities now. People talk about you behind your back. It was all well and good being a man of mystery when you first came to Paris, but you are to be a husband and father. You need—"

"A husband, certainly," Larten interrupted. "Never a father. You are more of a father to Gavner than I will ever be."

Tanish paused. Larten had never told Tanish why he treated Gavner so bluntly. Unlike Alicia, Tanish had an idea – vampires were careful drinkers, but sometimes one made a mistake and killed by accident, and he thought this had happened to Larten with one of the boy's parents – but Larten had never discussed the specifics with him. He thought it was a shame that Larten was denying himself the joys of fatherhood – Tanish would have loved a boy like Gavner to call his own – but he knew better than to provoke the fiery vampire. Larten had a short temper and could bear a grudge a long time when angered.

"You might not play the full role of a father," Tanish said cautiously, "but you must assume at least some of the attributes. Gavner thinks of Alicia as his mother. When you become her husband, you must stand as a stepfather to him. You might not love the boy, but I don't think you wish to shame him, do you?"

"Shame him?" Larten barked. "I have never done anything to shame Gavner."

"Not yet, but when you become his father, at least in the eyes of others," he added quickly before Larten growled at him again, "you'll be expected to go to his school every so often to watch him on the sporting field and discuss his future with his teachers. When he makes friends, their parents will want to dine with you and Alicia. It's the way things work. You were able to keep out of that social loop before, but your situation has changed. You'll need to change too.

"It won't help Gavner if these rumors about you continue unchecked," Tanish said softly. "He already comes in for criticism and bullying, but when you marry Alicia and become his official father, that will worsen."

"I never heard of Gavner being bullied," Larten said, troubled.

"He tells me things that he doesn't share with you," Tanish said. "Gavner is struggling to fit in at school. People mistrust him because they are suspicious of you. Unless you actively dislike the boy and enjoy watching him suffer, you must reconsider the way you behave towards him."

Larten was silent a long time, mulling over Tanish's words. When Alicia came back with wine and ale – and a tray of sandwiches for the ever peckish Tanish – she saw Larten's worried look and asked if everything was well.

"Aye," he sighed. "Tanish has asked me to go into business with him." Alicia stared at him and Tanish raised an eyebrow, sensing victory. Larten looked at both of them flatly, then smiled and said, "I have decided to accept."

Although the pair cheered and toasted him, he struggled to maintain the smile. Because, even allowing for all the good reasons that Tanish had set before him, Larten felt that he had made a poor call and was embarking on a dangerous path. He had an uneasy sense that destiny was steering him astray once again.

Chapter Eight

There was much more to running a casino than Larten had imagined. Croupiers had to be watched like a hawk or they'd rob the house blind. Dancers had to be kept in shape and choreographed. The ladies who frequented the areas around the tables had to be vetted and monitored. There were all sorts of tradesmen to deal with, officials to bribe, overheads to settle.

"Charna's guts!" Larten exclaimed at the end of his first week. "This is no fit work for a vampire. Let us burn your casinos to the ground and take off for the wilds." He was only half joking.

Tanish dealt with Larten's outbursts calmly. He had a smooth way of taking the sting out of any situation. He let Larten rant and rave, then soothed him with a joke or focused his attention elsewhere. He kept his old friend away from certain areas of the business – such as the opium dens he operated – knowing he wouldn't approve. Larten was for the most part a moral man. In time, as he learned more about the business and developed a taste for money and power, those morals would loosen and Tanish could lead him into seedier ventures. For now, though, it was better to pretend that he was halfway honest.

Tanish didn't wish to corrupt Larten. If anyone had accused him of being a bad influence on the other vampire, he would have reacted with genuine astonishment. He only wanted to get closer to his friend and build strong bonds between them, so that he needn't feel so alone at the center of the web that he had woven for himself since turning his back on the clan.

Alicia knew nothing about Tanish's dark secrets. She saw his positive features – the way he brought light into the lives of Larten and Gavner – and turned a deaf ear to rumors of his faults, dismissing them as she dismissed those about her fiancé. But she sensed that Larten wasn't completely sure of his decision and told him he could withdraw from the partnership any time he wanted.

"I'll love you no matter what you do," she said late one night when he came back bleary-eyed and low of spirits. "You don't have to prove yourself to me, and you don't have to support me. I'm a woman of wealth, remember?"

Alicia had money of her own, but they hadn't spent much of it since he'd begun to court her. Larten was old-fashioned and believed a man should pay for everything. Alicia thought that was ridiculous, but she let him have his way and left her money sitting in the bank, only spending what he earned.

"We have had that argument before," Larten grunted sourly.

"I know. And I thought it was behind us. But I'd rather we drew from my reserves than you come home unhappy all the time. I would spend every last franc in my account before I'd see you sad, my darling."

Larten smiled at that and kissed her. "I am not sad," he said. "It is just a shock, all this honest work. I am not accustomed to it. Once I adjust, I will be fine. I simply need more time."

If circumstances hadn't conspired against him,

perhaps Larten would have acclimatized to his new position. Maybe he would have succumbed to the cheap, tempting pleasures of the human world, and all would have been different with him and those he loved. But a few nights after his conversation with Alicia, he paid a surprise visit to one of Tanish's casinos, and what he discovered changed everything.

Larten was checking the stock of whiskey in a club before it opened for business when an angry man pounded on the door and demanded to speak with Tanish Eul. The manager tried to turn him away, but Larten was curious and told him to let the gentleman in.

"Who are you?" the man snarled when he was presented to Larten.

"Vur Horston," Larten replied. "I am Monsieur Eul's partner. Can I help you?"

"I want the organ grinder, not the monkey," the man barked.

Larten's face darkened and he leaned forward menacingly. "Do you wish to apologize for that ill-advised remark, sir?"

The man stared at Larten's burning eyes and the

scar on his left cheek. Gulping, he smiled weakly and said, "Please forgive me. I spoke hastily."

Larten nodded and gestured to a chair. As the man sat, Larten asked for his name. "Maurice Fabris," he introduced himself.

"How can I be of help, Monsieur Fabris?"

"I'm not sure that you can. It's that rogue Eul I want. But if you're his partner, perhaps you can be of some use...."

Maurice Fabris spoke quickly and plainly. Tanish had introduced him to a number of lady friends over the years. A few had stolen small items on occasion – that was something he expected – but the latest had taken a watch of great value, along with all of the money in his wallet. He'd been trying to track her down, but had enjoyed no success. He hadn't been able to find Tanish either, and he had the sense he was being deliberately avoided.

"The money's not so important," Maurice said, "but I can't replace the watch. It was a gift from my wife, and she will want to know where it is."

"Leave this matter with me, monsieur," Larten said, looking solemn but smiling inside. This would be a welcome break from the more monotonous work of the casino. He'd find the girl, sort this out and impress Tanish. "If I could just have her name?"

The girl was called Beatrice. Larten asked for a description of her too, since a lot of the ladies in Tanish's employ went by more than one name. Armed with that, he promised to investigate the matter fully. He would do all in his power to return the watch, he said, and if he failed he would compensate Monsieur Fabris for twice its value. That satisfied the irate customer, and once he'd left, Larten set off in pursuit of the elusive Beatrice.

Larten had a good memory for faces, and when Maurice described the girl – five foot two, long blond hair, blue eyes, a faint scar over her right eye, missing a tooth near the front of her mouth – he placed her instantly. There'd been a dancer like that in one of the clubs a few months ago and he had seen her again more recently, this time doing the rounds in one of Tanish's casinos.

Larten hailed a cab and went directly to the casino. It was early, but there were a few customers already hard at it, gambling solemnly and without pleasure, creatures of addiction rather than casual merrymakers.

The staff on duty nodded politely to Larten as he entered. Larten bowed in reply, then went upstairs to search for Beatrice. You could usually find the ladies on the casino floor, but their customers wouldn't arrive until later, so most were relaxing.

Larten found several women in a large room, sipping wine and chatting softly. They looked worried – almost scared – when he opened the door without warning and entered. But when they saw who it was, they smiled—all of them liked the courteous, serious, orange-haired charmer.

"Good afternoon, Monsieur Horston," a lady who went by the name of Charlotte greeted him. "Can we help you with anything?"

A few of the girls tittered, but Larten ignored them. "Is Tanish here?"

"No, monsieur. I haven't seen him for three or four days."

"What about Beatrice?" As soon as he mentioned her name the smile vanished from Charlotte's face. The others also went dumb. "What is wrong?" Larten asked as Charlotte glanced away. "Do you know where she is?"

"No, monsieur," Charlotte said quietly.

"She is not in any trouble," Larten said. "At least she will not be if I can find her. She stole a watch from a gentleman, but I can rectify the situation, even if she has sold it. I will not punish her. If you tell me where she is, I promise—"

"But I don't know!" Charlotte cried, then buried her face in her arms and wept.

As Larten stared at Charlotte, astonished, another woman – he didn't know her name – said, "Beatrice isn't hiding, monsieur. She has vanished. Three others are missing too."

"Missing?" Larten frowned.

"They've disappeared," the woman said.

"No—they've been *taken*," Charlotte corrected her, looking up again. "Killed, I'm sure. And any one of us could be next." The other ladies moaned and bunched together for comfort.

"What makes you think they have been killed?" Larten asked.

"It's not the first time," Charlotte said. "It has happened before. To…" She gulped and looked at the others for support. When they nodded, she added in a hushed voice, "To women who work for Tanish Eul."

Larten's eyes narrowed. "Are you making an accusation against Tanish?"

"No," Charlotte groaned. "Monsieur Eul has always been good to us. He pays us well and treats us kindly. But this happened seven or eight years ago, and there are rumors it happened before that too. Several of the women working for him dropped out of sight and were never heard from again."

"This is madness," Larten snapped, advancing furiously. "How dare you spread such rumors about…"

He caught sight of something and came to a stunned halt. He stared for a long moment at the lady who had spoken when Charlotte turned away to weep. Then he asked softly, "What is your name, madame?"

"Ginette," she answered, holding his gaze although she was trembling.

"I will deal with this, Ginette," Larten said firmly. "Monsieur Eul is not the guilty party. You have nothing to fear from him. I will find the abductor – the *killer* – and I will stop him. You have my word."

Ginette looked at Larten for a long time, then smiled hopefully. "I don't know why, but I believe you, monsieur."

"Stay together for the next few nights," Larten said. "Keep the others close too. I will tell you when it is safe again."

He spun on his heel and exited. As he hurried down the stairs, he thought again of what he'd seen.

Ginette was a pretty young woman with pale, smooth skin. But there were marks on her left cheek, three small scratches, each the same length. She probably thought that she had scratched herself in her sleep, but Larten knew better.

Ginette had been marked for death by a vampaneze.

Chapter Nine

Larten spent more than three hours searching for Tanish, frantically aware that if the vampaneze had struck four times already, he might have marked others besides Ginette and could even now be moving in for the kill. Larten hadn't much personal experience with the purple-skinned killers, but he knew they normally marked their victims in advance, three small scratches on the left cheek, a night or two before they planned to strike.

Larten finally tracked down Tanish in one of his smaller casinos. The overweight vampire was gambling with a few of his wealthier friends at a private table. The stakes were high, but nobody was taking the game too seriously. Tanish only gambled with men who didn't mind losing, for whom betting was a sport, not a way of life.

Larten waited for a break in the game – he didn't want to let the others see his agitation – then called Tanish aside. Tanish sensed something awry, but he never let his smile slip. Telling the others to carry on, he slid into a room at the rear of the establishment and closed the door after Larten had edged in behind him.

"What's wrong?" Tanish asked, taking a seat and snorting a pinch of snuff.

"Trouble," Larten said bluntly, then quickly told him what had happened.

Tanish listened silently. He was quiet for a few seconds when Larten finished. Then he cursed angrily. "I told Beatrice to stop stealing. Lots of the girls take trinkets, a ring here, a few coins there, but she was greedy. I've avoided Maurice since I heard what he was looking for. I hoped he'd simply tell his wife that he lost the damn watch." He cursed again, then sighed. "But I have only myself to blame. I should have dismissed her from my service, but I was fond of her. The mistake was mine, not hers."

"What are you talking about?" Larten snapped.

"This is far more important than a stolen watch. A vampaneze is on the loose and targeting women who work for you." Larten was striding up and down in front of the seated Tanish, thinking out loud. "It is strange that he goes after women working in the same place. They are usually more cunning than that. He might be insane – apparently the vampaneze let their mad live – but the girls say that this happened before and the bodies were never found. This is bizarre. I cannot understand it."

"I can," Tanish said and there was an almost merry lilt to his tone.

Larten stopped and stared at his friend. Now that he thought about it, he realized that Tanish had reacted too calmly. He hadn't been shocked. There was no alarm in his expression or concern for his employees in his eyes.

"Do you remember Randel Chayne?" Tanish asked casually.

"No," Larten said, then blinked as a memory surfaced. "Wait. That was the vampaneze who challenged us when we were Cubs, the one who..."

"...killed Zula Pone," Tanish finished when Larten stalled. "A nasty piece of work. He hated vampires. Still does. There has always been bad blood between the clans, but some, like Randel and our old friend Wester, bear more of a grudge than the rest of us."

"You think this is Randel Chayne's work?" Larten asked.

"I don't think it's Randel," Tanish said. "I *know* it is." He smirked at Larten's incredulous look. "Randel came upon me by chance several years after I'd left the clan. I was in a different city then, though my line of business was much the same as now. When Randel found me living as a human, he was disgusted. He waylaid me one night and challenged me to a duel. He said I was an insult even to the bad name of the vampires, but he would give me a chance to die nobly.

"As you might imagine, I was none too keen on that and refused his challenge. I thought he was going to kill me anyway, but he let me live and instead focused on those who worked for me. He slaughtered several of my pretty things, along with a few of my business associates.

"I fled, thinking that would be the end of it. But Randel followed me from city to city, always finding me and tormenting those I was close to. Eventually I settled here and when he came – as I knew he would – I let him kill until he grew tired of it. It was bad for business, of course, but at least he hid the bodies. A few people linked the disappearances to me, but I had alibis, and when he moved on they let the matter drop. After all, nobody of any real importance had been killed."

Larten was listening with a growing sense of horror. He knew Tanish had a low opinion of humans, as many vampires did, but he'd never suspected him of being this detached. Tanish could have been talking about cattle or sheep.

"I hoped that was the end of our unhealthy relationship," Tanish continued, "but Randel returned years later and again killed some of my pretty things, along with others who worked for me. And now he has come again. He's persistent, I'll grant him that."

Tanish laughed as if it was a joke, but Larten saw nothing funny in it. "This cannot continue," Larten growled. "He is killing *people*, Tanish."

Tanish shrugged. "It's what the vampaneze do. They always kill when they feed, and we let them. Anything for peace, aye?"

"This is different," Larten snapped. "Vampaneze of good standing only kill when they need to, a victim every month or so. But Randel has already murdered four times. How many more before he loses interest and moves on again?"

"Maybe ten or twelve," Tanish said lightly. "But you're right. This can't go on. People are gossiping. I thought they'd forget the earlier murders, but humans must have better memories than I gave them credit for. Perhaps it's time to leave Paris and settle somewhere new again. What do you think of Moscow?"

"You cannot be serious," Larten gasped.

"Too cold?" Tanish frowned.

"I am not talking about Moscow!" Larten roared, then lowered his voice in case he drew attention. "We have to kill him or drive him away."

"Are you mad?" Tanish yelped. "Vampires never interfere with the vampaneze. We have a treaty, remember? They feed as they please and we keep out of their way. We'd draw every vampaneze in Europe down on us if we went after Randel."

"No," Larten said. "He is not feeding naturally. He is doing this to torment you, meaning he was the first to take action. We would simply be reacting, as we would to a challenge."

"I don't think the vampaneze would see it that way," Tanish said.

"It does not matter. We have to put a stop to this, whatever the risks. He has marked Ginette. We cannot stand by and let him kill her."

"Why not?" Tanish asked. "I don't know the girl that well. You don't either. What does it matter if he kills her? She's human. She'll die soon enough anyway."

Larten started to argue, then realized he'd be wasting his breath. Spitting on the floor to show his contempt, he turned to leave.

"Vur!" Tanish squealed. "*Larten*. Stop, I beg you, and think. We have a beautiful setup here. Having to move is a nuisance, but we'll prosper wherever we wind up. You have a good job, money coming in, enough to support Alicia in the style to which she's accustomed and secure a fine education for Gavner.

"The women Randel is killing...they're nothing. Cheap, low-class, worthless. Let him end their short lives a few decades earlier than scheduled. What of it? The world won't have lost much. But if you get in Randel's way, you could lose it all—your position, my friendship, Alicia's love. Let this pass. We'll take a cruise, visit the pyramids. You'll forget about this in no time."

"Perhaps I would," Larten murmured without looking back. "But some things in life should not be forgotten." And he stormed out of the room without another word.

Chapter Ten

Larten longed to go home and tell Alicia what was happening, or at least bid her farewell in case he perished at the hands of Randel Chayne and never saw her again. But night had fallen and the vampaneze could strike at any moment. He could not afford to think about himself. So he returned to the casino and stood watch on a rooftop at the rear of the building.

There was no guarantee that Ginette would be Randel's next target, or that he would attack tonight even if she was. But she was Larten's only link to the killer. He could do nothing but shadow her and wait.

Larten thought about Tanish while he sat in darkness, hidden from the light of the moon behind a large brick chimney. He understood his friend's position. Larten had known for a long time that Tanish was a coward, but even if he hadn't been, he might have adopted a similar stance.

Many in the clan thought that humans were inferior. Few vampires would risk their lives for a human, especially one they had no personal ties to. Weakness wasn't respected in the vampire world. The main reason they didn't kill when they fed was to avoid trouble, not because they thought that all life was precious.

But Larten couldn't turn his back on this. If it had been ten years ago, before he lost his mind on the ship to Greenland and became a monster... perhaps. He liked to think he would have interceded even then, but he wasn't sure.

What he did know for certain was that he had changed. Too many innocents had died at his hands for him to remain neutral in a matter such as this. Maybe Tanish was right and it was madness, but Larten could no more let Randel go on killing freely than he could lie on a beach for a whole day without burning.

Larten also thought of Alicia and Gavner while he waited. They would suffer if he lost this fight, especially if Randel hid his remains and they never found out what had become of him. Alicia might think that he had lost interest in her and left to seek love elsewhere. He doubted Tanish would correct her. He had an inkling his cunning friend might even encourage such thoughts and try to win Alicia's love for himself.

If Larten had been able to write, he would have found a pen and paper and sent a message to Alicia. But being illiterate, he could only send his thoughts and pray she somehow received them.

"I must learn to read, if I get out of this alive," he muttered. "It is ridiculous, a man my age never having made the time to . . ."

He stopped. A skylight had opened and someone was crawling onto the casino roof, dragging a slumped figure. As the man shut the window behind him, Larten glimpsed a flash of purple skin. The vampaneze must have been in the casino already, hiding in a dark corner. Perhaps he'd slept there through the day, waiting for darkness, smelling Ginette even in his sleep.

Larten wished he had some of the throwing stars favored by Vancha March. Normally he'd face an opponent cleanly, one on one, but in this situation he would have happily struck down Randel from afar, without warning. But having only an ornamental knife, which he always carried, Larten had to wait for the vampaneze to leap from the roof of the casino to one closer to where he was stationed.

As soon as Randel landed, cushioning the unconscious Ginette on his shoulder, Larten attacked. He threw himself silently at the vampaneze, scampering across the roof like an agile cat. He would have struck unseen, if instinct hadn't made Randel pause and look back.

The vampaneze's eyes shot wide when he saw the vampire closing in on him. He dropped the woman and dug out a knife much larger than Larten's feeble blade.

Larten's momentum drove him into the vampaneze and the pair rolled silently across the roof, stabbing wildly at each other. Both connected, but neither was able to cut deeply or sever any major veins or arteries. Larten had the advantage, having landed on top of Randel, but then the vampaneze bit his neck and he had to pull away or risk his throat being torn open. The slight gap gave Randel the space to ram his knee into Larten's stomach and the vampire fell back, winded.

Randel was on his feet before Larten hit the roof.

He had no idea who his foe was or why he'd been attacked, and like any natural warrior he didn't care. Rather than waste time asking questions, he threw himself at his assailant and stabbed at his heart. He would rather live in ignorance than die well informed.

Larten blocked Randel's thrust, and instead of piercing his heart, the tip of the knife ended up stuck in a tile. Larten jammed his own knife into the vampaneze's thigh. Randel hissed and jerked his leg free. The blade snapped in half and Larten tossed the useless hilt away. He had trained to fight with his bare hands, so he wasn't overly concerned, particularly since Randel's knife remained wedged in the tile.

Larten got a hand between his face and Randel's and pushed. Randel tried to chew Larten's fingers, but the vampire was too experienced to be caught out like that. Seba, Vanez Blane and his other instructors had taught him to be wary of the dirty moves as well as the legitimate.

Sliding his fingers away from Randel's teeth, Larten jabbed at the vampaneze's eyes. He gouged one of them and Randel fell away, cursing. Larten followed like a flash of lightning, glad that his reflexes were as sharp as ever. If he won this battle, he'd be able to smile at his old nickname of Quicksilver and think how apt it had been. But this fight was far from won, and only a fool would congratulate himself while his opponent was still alive and dangerous.

Pinning Randel to the roof, Larten found the vampaneze's throat and squeezed. His fingers tightened and Randel's face turned an even darker shade of purple. A vampaneze could hold his breath far longer than a human, but Randel had been panting from the fight and hadn't much oxygen left in his lungs. He had to break his enemy's hold quickly or he was lost.

The desperate vampaneze worked an arm free and tugged at Larten's hand. When that didn't make a difference, he punched Larten's face, trying to smash his nose. Larten tucked his chin in tight and took the blows on his forehead, grunting but still in control. Randel tried to poke at the vampire's eyes but Larten was alert to that trick and snapped at the purple fingers. He caught one and almost chewed it off, but Randel jerked free before he could gnaw through the bone.

Randel was weakening. He had fought many times and knew when a fight was lost. He didn't give up – a vampaneze never willingly accepted defeat – but he started to make his peace with the gods. If he was to die tonight, at least he'd die with a clear conscience.

Randel didn't ask forgiveness for the humans he had killed – in his view they didn't count – but for the times he had been weak, when he'd let down his proud and demanding clan.

Larten sensed victory, but remained focused. Many battles were lost in the last few seconds, when the one with the upper hand grew overconfident and gave his opponent a chance to snatch victory from the jaws of defeat. Larten wouldn't make that mistake. Just another thirty seconds of pressure and Randel would be dead. Then he could return Ginette to the casino and –

Something hard connected with the back of Larten's head. He gave a cry of shock and pain, then slumped over, fingers loosening, eyes swimming. He tried to rise, but was again struck from behind. He blacked out, but not for long. When he came to, Randel was sitting up, rubbing the flesh of his throat, staring with suspicion at his savior, who was talking rapidly.

"…Quick, before he recovers. Kill him, I tell you! If he gets up, we're finished. I'm giving him to you. What more can I do? You want me to kill him myself? I won't. I'm not *that* soulless. Kill him now, before –"

"*Tanish?*" Larten wheezed.

There was a moment of silence, then Tanish cursed. "There! You waited too long. He's awake."

"And it's well that he is," Randel growled. "I would never kill a vampire in his sleep. Only a coward strikes an unconscious foe."

"Oh for the love of…" Tanish muttered. "Very well. He can defend himself now. Are you going to finish this, or would you rather I revived him with smelling salts and gave him a sword?"

"Why are you doing this?" Randel asked. Larten wanted to ask the same question, but his lips were numb and he couldn't form the words.

"Self-preservation," Tanish snapped. "Larten's my friend, but I value my life more than our friendship. If I let him kill you, revenge would be sharp and savage. Your fellow vampaneze would pursue me, and they wouldn't heed my innocent pleas once they'd tracked me down."

"You are without even a shred of honor," Randel sneered.

"Tell me something new," Tanish croaked, then glanced at Larten as he tried to rise. He got as far as his knees then collapsed. "Finish him," Tanish said coldly. "I know you love tormenting me, but this is too much. He tried to kill you. He struck when your back was turned. Are you going to let him get away with that?"

"Ordinarily, no," Randel said, getting to his feet. He looked down at the groggy vampire and nodded approvingly. "But I understand why he attacked me, and I hate him far less than I hate you." Randel laughed cruelly. "Besides, I want to see what happens when he recovers. You'll have a new tormentor, Tanish Eul, but I doubt he'll settle for killing those close to you. I suspect your nights are numbered, you obese and shameful cur."

Still laughing, Randel bolted. Within seconds he'd vanished, leaving a stunned Tanish stranded on the roof with the swiftly recovering Larten.

Gritting his teeth, Larten rolled onto his back and glared at his onetime friend. He spat out blood and took deep breaths, wishing his legs didn't feel so heavy. He expected Tanish to attack and braced himself to meet the challenge.

But Tanish didn't move. He was trembling. He pulled a handkerchief from a pocket and dabbed sweat from his jowls. Grinning weakly at Larten, he giggled hysterically. "What a mess," he moaned. "I told you not to do it. You should have listened. She" – he kicked the unconscious Ginette – "wasn't worth this. You've ruined us, and for what? A *human*." He snarled the word, as if it were foul.

Larten wanted to tell Tanish that the girl was worth a dozen of him, but his head was still a sickly swirl and the words wouldn't come.

Tanish stepped closer. He was carrying a thick plank of wood, the weapon he had clubbed Larten with. The fat vampire's face was clouded by shadows, only the whites of his eyes visible, glinting malevolently in the moonlight. Larten recalled how often Gavner had swung from this man's ludicrous mustache, the times he'd kissed Alicia's cheeks, the jokes he'd told so well. He wanted to hate Tanish, but he couldn't. He felt only pity and disgust.

Tanish raised the plank. A few good blows to Larten's skull would finish the job. Larten stiffened and waited for the end. Unlike Randel Chayne, he didn't pray to the gods. He still felt that he was undeserving of Paradise and believed any prayers would be thrown back in his face.

"You fool," Tanish moaned and Larten realized he was crying. "Why couldn't you let things be? I've been alone so long. I thought I'd found a true friend at last. The plans I had for us..." He shook his head and brought the plank slamming down on Larten's skull.

Larten shut his eyes instinctively and opened his mouth to howl a death cry. But the plank never connected. A confused second later, Larten squinted. Wood filled his vision. When he moved his head slightly, he saw that Tanish had stopped short. His hands were trembling and his face – now exposed by the rays of the moon – was twisted.

"I can't," he cried. "Curse your eyes, Quicksilver, but I can't." He threw the plank aside and staggered away. Larten pushed himself up and stared at Tanish, bewildered.

Tanish was breathing raggedly, looking left and right, thinking furiously. Then his gaze settled on the motionless Ginette and he fell steady. The change was swift and eerie. All expression faded from his face and his eyes went cold.

"No!" Larten gasped, understanding Tanish's intent. He tried to scramble to his feet, but he was in no state to stop the large but nimble vampire.

Tanish leaned over the unaware Ginette, laid a sharp, hard nail to her pale, soft throat, then tore across the folds of flesh. She shook in his arms as blood spurted. He ducked out of the way of the arcing blood, then moved her so that the spray spattered Larten, who was crawling towards them, whining like a dying dog.

Some of Ginette's blood struck Larten's eyes and he stopped to wipe them. When he looked again, Tanish was standing by the edge of the roof, Ginette held lengthways in his arms. "No," Larten groaned, but it made no difference now. Even if he could have hauled Tanish back, Ginette was already dead.

Tanish held out the remains of the damned, pretty girl, then dropped her. She hit the ground with a loud, wet sound, but Larten didn't hear that because Tanish was roaring. "Help!" he screamed. "Murder! He drank her blood and killed her! Vur Horston is a vampire! *Help!*"

Lights flickered in the windows around them, in the casino and other buildings. Lamps were trained in their direction from the street. Tanish danced by the roof's edge, shrieking, screaming murder, crying for help, flapping his arms, pointing at Larten, who was now on his knees.

"I will kill you," Larten growled, finally finding his feet. He staggered towards Tanish, who quickly drew away from the advancing vampire.

106

"Don't be an idiot," Tanish snapped. "You have to run. This is your only chance. If you stay, they'll execute you."

"I do not care," Larten snarled.

"Maybe not. But Alicia and Gavner will."

Larten hesitated. Others were yelling now. Someone had discovered Ginette's body in the alley. He had been sighted by dozens of people, some of whom worked in the casino and recognized him. Tanish hadn't needed to shout his name.

"Flee," Tanish urged him. "Your death will serve no purpose. I'd rather not see you butchered, even though I'd be safer if you were dead. Fly, fool, if not for your sake, then for Alicia and the boy."

"I will come back," Larten said softly, pointing at Tanish with a shaking finger. "I will track you down and slaughter you. I swear it on the souls of all who have died because of your cowardice."

"You'll have to look hard," Tanish chuckled bleakly. "I'm going to hide where even that accursed vampaneze can't find me. No more high life for Tanish Eul, not for the next few decades anyway. But look if you must. Seek me if it pleases you. I'll give you satisfaction if you track me down, a duel that will set hearts racing when they recount it in Vampire

Mountain. Only now, for the love of the gods and all you hold dear, *go!*"

Larten let his finger point accusingly at Tanish for another long second, then spat and spun away. People were already taking to the roofs, pitchforks, knives and other weapons in hand, closing in on the apparently heartless murderer. But Larten was faster than the humans. Before they could trap him, he slipped through the tightening net and streaked across the Paris skyline. This wasn't the first time he had fled from a mob, but never before had he run with such a bitter taste in his mouth, a bitterness that could only ever be sweetened by bloody, wretched, vicious revenge.

Chapter Eleven

Larten waited nervously in a giant shed on the outskirts of Paris. The shed belonged to Alberto Santos-
Dumont. The aircraft enthusiast hadn't heard of the
uproar and had happily granted Larten permission to
stay when he'd turned up a week earlier, claiming to
have had a disagreement with Alicia, asking for shelter. Alberto assumed Alicia had caught Larten with
another woman, and having tutted at such folly, he'd
returned to work on his beloved *bird of prey* and
barely taken any notice of Larten after that.

It had been a long, frustrating week. Larten knew
he was risking everything by staying, that he should
have carried on running. But he couldn't leave without

seeing Alicia. It might be for the last time, or maybe she'd accept him for what he was and travel onwards with him. Either way he had to speak with her. He couldn't let her go on thinking he was a killer.

When he felt that enough time had passed, he asked one of Alberto's assistants to carry a message to Alicia, telling her where he was and asking her to meet with him. He told the man to say that Larten would understand if she didn't want to come, but if she cared to see him, he would wait for her every day at midday for the next week.

She turned up on the fifth day, when he had all but given up hope. He smelled her before he heard or saw her. Brushing straw from his hair and clothes, he stood by the door and waited, close to the world of sunlight, aware that she might not want to come into the shed where it was dark.

Alicia had black rings under her eyes from crying. She looked like she hadn't slept since he'd last seen her. She was unusually scruffy and walked like an old woman. She stopped several feet shy of the door and stared at him. He couldn't read her expression.

"I did not kill Ginette," he said softly. No reply. "It was Tanish."

At that her eyes widened, then narrowed. "Tanish killed her?"

"Yes."

"Why?"

"Because he could not bring himself to kill *me*." When Alicia frowned, he explained the whole story. About vampires, the Cubs, Tanish's history with Randel Chayne, trying to save Ginette. Alicia listened in silence and thought about it at length once he'd finished.

"Why should I believe you?" she finally asked.

"Surely you know me well enough to know when I am telling the truth."

"I thought I did," she nodded. "But I never really knew you at all. I bet Vur Horston isn't even your real name, is it?"

"No," he admitted. "I am Larten Crepsley."

"And you're a vampire?"

"Aye. But not like the monster in the–"

"How long?" she interrupted. "How long have you been like *this*?"

"I was blooded a century or so ago," he said.

She looked like she was about to be sick. "You're a hundred years old?"

"Give or take a few years." He tried to smile. "I look good for my age, aye?"

"Gavner!" she cried. "Don't tell me he's one too!"

"Gavner is an ordinary boy," Larten calmed her. "Vampires cannot have children, and I never blooded him. I was tempted to, when we were adrift in Greenland and his life was endangered, but we prefer to blood those who can make the choice for themselves."

"Greenland?" Alicia echoed weakly.

"That is a story for another time. Unless this is our last..." He couldn't go on. He wanted to rush to her, hold her, hug her, kiss her. But he had no right. This was a woman he loved but had lied to. He'd promised to marry her without telling her who he really was, that he'd long outlive her, that he couldn't father the children she craved. What right had he to expect anything of her now?

"Have you seen Tanish?" he asked instead.

Alicia shook her head. "He left the next morning. He said he feared for his life and urged me to leave with him. He said that Gavner and I wouldn't be safe while you were on the loose. I wanted to go – it's been horrible, people look at us with hatred and suspicion, as if we're to blame for what happened to that poor woman – but I couldn't. I knew you wouldn't harm us and I sensed you hadn't run far. I had to wait, to give you a chance to explain."

"And now that I have?" he asked quietly.

Alicia's face contorted. "Why didn't you tell me?" she shouted. "You let me fall in love with you. I thought we could have a life together, but all the time you were sneaking off at night, drinking blood, mocking me behind my back."

"Never," Larten growled. "My love was true, even if little else was. The proposal of marriage was a mistake, but it was an error of the heart. I forgot what I was. In your arms I believed the lies. I thought..." He shook his head miserably.

"But you did drink," she said stiffly. "You cut people open and swallowed their blood."

"Small amounts," he said. "I never hurt them. We do not kill when we feed. I told you that."

"But maybe you're lying again. How can I believe anything you say?"

Larten hung his head. There was no answer to that.

Alicia was crying. She said nothing until she had her tears under control. Larten was silent too, waiting in the shadows of the shed, not separated from her by the sun but by a wall of bitter lies. "We're finished," she said eventually, and he felt his heart tighten. "I can never take you back. You know that, don't you?"

"Aye," he sighed.

"Even if I wanted to, if I went with you and accepted your unnatural appetites and all the rest, it wouldn't be fair to Gavner. You gave him to me to raise and told me I must do my best for him. I wouldn't be doing that if I exposed him to a life of darkness and blood."

"But if not for Gavner...?" He wasn't sure why he asked. Better to think there had never been any hope of happiness than to believe he might have had her, if not for the boy.

"I don't know," Alicia moaned. "Perhaps."

Larten nodded sourly. He had often thought that he deserved to be punished for what he'd done on the ship. Now it seemed that fate had got around to dealing with him at last. The boy whom he'd orphaned had ended up denying him any chance of love from the woman he adored. It was fitting in its way.

"Where will you go?" she asked.

"Wherever Tanish has scuttled off to," he growled.

"You're going to hunt him?"

"Aye." Larten's hands balled into angry fists. He could have forgiven the cowardice, the selfishness, even the betrayal. But he'd never forget the way Tanish had slit Ginette's throat and casually dropped her from the roof.

Alicia hesitated, then said, "I wish you wouldn't."

Larten was shocked. "After what I told you?" he barked. "Tanish let people die. He offered me to the vampaneze and killed Ginette. You want me to allow him to trot away, lie low for a while, then build a new empire for himself?"

"I make no excuses for Tanish," Alicia said. "He meant more to you than he ever did to me. But Gavner loves him. Tanish was the father that you refused to be. If you kill him and Gavner finds out, he will hate you and maybe even hunt you down to seek revenge. If he does, one of you will surely die, and that would tear me apart. I beg you, Vur – *Larten*, if that's your real name – if you ever loved me, do me this favor and don't seek revenge on Tanish Eul. Please."

Larten hadn't thought about Gavner and his feelings for the sly vampire. He was sure, if Alicia explained it to the boy, that Gavner would understand. But perhaps the child shouldn't be told. He would learn the true nature of the world as he grew up, but he deserved this period of innocence and faith in the goodness of man. It would be wrong to expose him to the ugly truth at such a tender age.

115

But at the same time there were scores to be settled, debts to pay, deaths to account for.

"I will let Tanish be for now," Larten said gruffly. "I will not move against him while Gavner is a boy. But when he is a man, there will come a time of reckoning, and I will move on Tanish regardless of the consequences. Ask no more of me, for this is as much as I will promise. And I would promise it to none other than you."

Alicia bit her lip, seemed about to argue with him, then nodded curtly. "Thank you." She turned to leave and his heart sank. But then she stopped and glanced back. "Was your love truly real?" she asked softly.

"Truly," he whispered.

"So was mine," she wept, then fled, wiping fresh tears from her cheeks.

Larten watched the woman he loved flee from him, taking all of his hopes and dreams with her. When she was gone, he slowly closed the door of the shed and retreated. He didn't think of Alicia – he knew she would fill his thoughts for many nights and years to come – but instead focused on his immediate future. He didn't want to let this destroy him, and if he sat here, moping, he was sure that it would. He needed to move on, put this chapter of his life behind

116

him, make a new start and try to build yet again. But where to go when the sun went down? It was a wide world and all areas were open to him.

The answer came before he had finished asking the question. Larten had made many mistakes in the past and gone far astray. He'd been a wanderer, a killer, a lover. He had tried to be human and he had failed. For years he'd roamed without real purpose, denying his true calling, torn between two worlds, able to commit to neither.

Now at last he was ready to put humanity behind him forever. If the Generals and Princes accepted him, he would return to the clan and pledge himself to their cause for however long the gods gave him. It was time to face Seba, Wester and Vampire Mountain again.

It was time to go home.

Part Three

"beloved red"

Chapter Twelve

Larten encountered no other vampires on his way to the mountain, and he was glad of that. The months alone in the wilderness sharpened his skills and senses. It had been a long time since he'd lived like a true vampire and he found the harsh isolation refreshing. He was haunted by thoughts of Alicia and Tanish, plagued by a locust swarm of regrets. But Seba had always said that the past could never be changed and only a fool fretted about it, so he tried his best not to dwell on his mistakes and losses.

But it was hard.

At least he'd left his doubts behind. As he abandoned the day world completely – only rising each night when the sun had firmly set – and hunted once more as a vampire, he realized he genuinely loved this life. He couldn't wait to see the peak of Vampire Mountain and drink bat broth again. He wanted to catch up with all the news, complete his training, assume his place as a General. His uncertainty had vanished—forever, he hoped. He had put his human longings behind him and could face the future as a committed night creature now.

Of course there was a strong possibility that it would be a very short future. When the Princes heard of his crimes on the ship they might sentence him to death. If that was the case, he would accept their verdict without argument, as any true vampire would, and do his best to die cleanly and with honor.

His breath caught in his throat when he finally sighted the snowcapped mountain one cold, blustery night. It stood ahead of him like a beacon, drawing him home. It had been a long time since he drank fresh blood, and he'd been sipping sparingly from his bottles for the last few weeks, so he wasn't at his strongest. Even so, he picked up the pace and jogged the last stretch. It should have been a two-night trek, but he was determined to reach the mountain by dawn, and he did.

Larten slept for a few hours when he made the shelter of one of the tunnels leading into the mountain. Revived, he climbed swiftly, following the carved signs on the walls, smiling eagerly in the gloom. It was the first time he'd smiled since Paris.

He hoped Wester would be on duty at the gate – it would make for a startling reunion – but he didn't recognize the man in green garb. The guard was surprised to see the orange-haired vampire, but once he took Larten's name and checked the scars on his fingertips, he let him pass.

Larten made for the Hall of Osca Velm. It was virtually deserted, as most of the Halls were in the long years between Councils. It would liven up later, when the young vampires in training rose to prepare for another grueling set of lessons. But for now it was almost a ghost Hall.

Larten helped himself to some stale bread and cold cuts of meat. He ate slowly and washed down the food with water from one of the mountain streams. He was nervous now that the time had come to face his old companions. He wasn't sure what sort of welcome to expect. What if Seba didn't want to see him, if he turned his ex-assistant away like a rabid hound?

Larten almost retreated. He was seriously considering going back the way he'd come, to perish in the snow, when he became aware of someone standing behind him. Looking around, he found an ancient, wrinkled, gray-haired vampire dressed entirely in red.

"I have been waiting for you," Seba said softly.

"How did you know I was coming?" Larten gasped. "Did you search for me with the Stone of Blood?"

"I did not need to," Seba said, his voice cracking. "How could I not know you were near when I could feel you" – he pressed a hand to his chest – "here?"

He held out his arms and Larten hurled himself into them, hugging his mentor hard, blinking back tears, his fears of rejection vanishing like the foolish wisps of fancy they had always been.

The pair of vampires sat, heads close together, for many hours, discussing all that Larten had endured since he'd parted ways with his master. Elements of Larten's story saddened Seba, but didn't surprise him. The quartermaster had seen and heard pretty much everything in his six hundred years. Larten's tale wasn't so different from that of dozens of others who had lost their way for a while.

But Seba was genuinely shocked when Larten said

that he had discovered Perta Vin-Grahl's palace of coffins. Seba made him describe it several times, listening like an entranced child. He was troubled by talk of Desmond Tiny — it was never a good sign when that infernal meddler showed an interest in a person — but he tried not to let that overshadow Larten's remarkable find.

"This is a momentous occasion," Seba insisted. "Many vampires have set out in search of those tombs of ice, and all have failed. This will stand you in good stead at the next Council. But I fear you will have to repeat your story more times than you might wish to."

Larten sighed. "Maybe I will only have to repeat it once. When I tell the Princes what happened on the ship…"

"There is only one Prince in residence," Seba said. "He has little time for those who stray from the path, but I am sure he will judge you fairly."

"Which Prince is it?" Larten asked.

"He is new to the throne," Seba said. "A couple of the older Princes have died since you left. This is the first of their replacements. There will be more in the not-so-distant future, but so far—"

"Is Paris Skyle one of the dead?" Larten interrupted, thinking for a horrible moment that the elderly Prince – a hundred years older than Seba – had passed on to Paradise in his absence.

"No," Seba chuckled. "Sire Skyle is still going strong. I think he will live to be a thousand." The quartermaster stood and groaned, rubbing the small of his back. "Come, I will present you to our noble new leader."

"Who is he?" Larten asked, but Seba only touched his nose and winked.

"What about Wester?" Larten muttered as they made their way to the Hall at the top of the mountain. "I would like to see him before I introduce myself to the Prince, in case things go badly and I am executed."

"I doubt that will happen," Seba said. "In any case, if the luck of the vampires is with us, we might run into Master Flack along the way."

Larten kept an eye out for Wester, but saw no sign of him. He was disappointed, but said nothing as they approached the tunnel that led to the Hall of Princes. He would have to seek out Wester later, the verdict of the new Prince permitting.

A slender guard stepped into their way as they neared the tunnel. No weapons were allowed beyond this point. Guards always checked those who wished to pass, even the quartermaster. There would be a body search and their hair would be combed for hidden blades.

"I wasn't expecting you tonight," the thin guard said to Seba. Then he saw Larten and his jaw dropped. Larten's dropped too. They gasped each other's name at the same moment.

"Larten?"

"Wester?"

Larten lunged forward and picked up the lighter vampire. He swung him around with delight and Wester whooped. The pair were brothers in all ways but birth. It was only now that they'd been reunited that Larten realized how much he had missed his best friend.

"Look at you!" Larten exclaimed, releasing Wester and admiring his outfit. "A guard of the Hall of Princes."

"It will do until something better comes along," Wester joked. This was the highest honor for any of the mountain's guards. Only the most respected and trusted were granted the privilege of guarding the entrance to the throne room. Larten had never thought that Wester would achieve such a lofty position so early in his career, but he was delighted for him. Proud too. His own future didn't seem so important now that he'd seen how well Wester was doing.

"Where have you been?" Wester asked. "What have you been up to? Why have you returned?"

"He will explain all later," Seba said calmly. "First I must present him to the Prince. If you will let us pass..."

Seba started forward. A split second later, the tip of Wester's sword was at his master's throat. "No farther, old man," Wester chuckled, but he was serious too. He knew that Seba was only playing with him, but if the ancient vampire actually tried to pass without being searched, Wester would strike him dead in an instant, despite the fact that he loved the quartermaster as a father. He had been well trained and Larten was impressed by his quick hand and steely determination.

Seba stepped back and subjected himself to Wester's search. Three other guards watched closely. The Hall of Princes housed the Stone of Blood. Every vampire let the Stone absorb some of their blood when they joined the clan. It allowed any one of them to be located by a user of the Stone in an instant. If an enemy ever got their hands on it, they could use the Stone to track down and destroy practically every living vampire. The guards here took their duty *very* seriously.

When Seba and Larten had been cleared, Wester led them through the tunnel and into the Hall, where a large white dome gleamed warmly and pulsed eerily. Mr. Tiny had given the dome to the clan as a gift, along with the Stone of Blood. The vampires had been suspicious of the gifts to begin with, but now they were a sacred part of their culture.

Wester struck the doors to the dome four times with a staff he carried especially for this task. There was a pause, then the doors swung open. Wester made the death's touch sign and bid Larten luck.

"Are you not coming in to listen to my tale?" Larten asked.

"I can't," Wester said. "I'm on watch for another five hours. But I'll hear it later, if you don't mind telling it again."

"If the Prince lets me live, I will happily tell it as many times as you like," Larten said gloomily.

Wester was alarmed by that, but before he could ask any questions, Seba nudged Larten ahead of him, into the Hall where his fate would be decided.

Larten had only been inside the Hall of Princes once before, when he'd laid hands on the red Stone of

Blood and let it drain some of his blood, thus linking him forever to the clan. He paused as the doors closed, glanced at the bright walls – light came from them, though no vampire knew how – then at the thrones in the center of the room and the Stone of Blood on the pedestal behind them. He felt the way religious humans did in cathedrals or mosques.

Then he saw the new Prince, sitting awkwardly on one of the thrones, and his sense of awe evaporated, to be replaced by incredulous delight. "*Vancha?*" he cried.

A filthy vampire in purple skins, encircled by belts of throwing stars, raised an eyebrow and sat up straight. Brushing green hair back from his face, he said archly, "That's Sire Vancha, if you please." Then he winked, spat over an arm of the throne, broke wind loudly and grinned. "I bet you never saw this one coming!"

Chapter Thirteen

Vancha joked with Larten about his promotion for a while, but when he heard what had happened on the ship, he became a different person. Larten hadn't seen much of Vancha's serious side in the past. He'd initially thought that the scruffy General was an odd choice for a Prince, but as Vancha coolly discussed the killings with him, he came to see that the strange-looking vampire could judge as thoughtfully and wisely as Paris Skyle or any of the other Princes.

"You did wrong," Vancha said. "You were in a perilous situation, and they shouldn't have killed the girl, but slaughtering them all..."

"I know," Larten replied softly. "I make no plea for mercy."

"And that's the only reason I'm thinking of granting it," Vancha grunted. "We all make mistakes, though rarely as grave as yours. Those of good standing admit their errors and try to learn from them. Our laws are harsh, necessarily so, but they make certain allowances for those who are genuinely repentant."

He debated the matter with Seba, considered it at length, then finally said that he would grant Larten pardon. "But you'll have to atone for your sins eventually," he added. "Destiny will probably place you in a situation at some point where you must risk all and maybe suffer greatly to help a group of humans. But if it doesn't, you should look for such a group. Saving one life doesn't excuse the taking of another – the universe doesn't balance out so neatly – but it's a start."

Vancha was outraged when he learned of Tanish's treachery. He wanted to send a team of Generals to track down Tanish and make an example of him, but Larten begged for a stay of execution. "I would like to settle matters with Tanish myself," he said. "I made a promise not to kill him in the near future, so I ask that you leave his fate in my hands."

Vancha looked uneasy. "But if he murders others…"

"I do not think that he will," Larten said. "If he does, I will answer for those and you can punish me in his place."

Vancha wasn't happy, but he knew how important personal promises were, so he vowed to set the Tanish Eul matter aside and move against him only if Larten died or hesitated too long.

After that they chatted as old friends do when they haven't seen each other for years. Vancha told Larten about his investiture and what it felt like to be a Prince—he made it sound like more of a nuisance than an honor. Larten asked about Paris Skyle and his other friends. Vancha made him tell them again about the palace of Perta Vin-Grahl. Then the ugly Prince told him to find quarters, settle down and get a good day's sleep. "You can resume your training at sunset," he said.

And that was that. Larten was part of the clan once more, and life continued as if he'd never been away.

The next several years swept by in a busy blur. Larten worked hard, passed all the tests he was given, and at last was appointed a vampire General. It was a proud night when Paris Skyle – back at Vampire Mountain after his most recent adventures – pricked his thumb and daubed Larten's head with his Princely blood, the closing part of a long, complex ceremony.

Seba and Wester were present and they applauded softly, not wishing to appear overly enthusiastic, since this was a solemn occasion. But both had to wipe tears from their eyes when no one was looking, and afterwards they toasted Larten's name repeatedly until the barrels of ale in Vampire Mountain threatened to run dry.

Being a General wasn't that different than being an ordinary vampire, at least not for the first few years. Larten carried on with his regular duties. He often sparred with Vanez Blane and the other tutors to hone his skills. He worked with some of the younger vampires, teaching them the ways of the clan, but he wasn't a natural mentor and avoided such tasks when he could. He left the mountain every now and then to hunt in the wilds around it. Paris and Vancha sought his opinion on some minor issues that had been brought before them – judging his sense of judgment – and he got to vote with the rest of the Generals, which wasn't often, since the majority of voting issues were set aside for Council. But for the most part, things rolled along the same as ever.

Larten didn't mind. He knew that he would be given a mission sooner or later, and that he'd end up missing the peace of Vampire Mountain when called upon to leave it. His years of lonely wandering had taught him the importance of friends and stability. He was no longer in a rush to experience the cut and thrust of the outside world. Action and intrigue would find him if that was his destiny. And if they didn't, he would consider himself one of the lucky ones. There was much to be said for the quiet life.

Larten was glumly confident that fate didn't have a non-eventful future in store for him, so he cherished those dull, slow years. While destiny lined up whatever it planned to throw at him next, he trained, learned, lived cleanly and waited calmly.

Council came around again and Larten helped prepare the mountain for the influx of vampires. As a General he was expected to take control of situations, and he had a team of young vampires working under him. The responsibility alarmed him to begin with – life was a lot easier when someone else was giving the orders – but he adjusted quickly and was soon dealing smoothly with the variety of chores thrust his way by Seba, Vanez and others.

Larten developed a new level of respect for Seba and his role as quartermaster. The elderly vampire was kept on the go every waking minute and seldom got more than three hours' sleep a day, even less the closer they drew to the great gathering. He had to be in a dozen places at once, deal with a hundred panicking vampires, oversee everything.

It was an incredible juggling act. Seba delegated artfully, but there was much that he had to personally tend to. Larten doubted that he would ever have the experience or patience to cope with a job like this. He didn't envy his old master and was glad that it was highly unlikely that he would ever be offered the post of quartermaster. Wester was far more suited to a job like that, and as far as Larten was concerned, he was more than welcome to it.

The first vampires began arriving for Council a few months before it began. There was never a set date for the Festival of the Undead. It would begin once all who were coming were present.

About a month before the big night, Larten spotted Mika Ver Leth on his way to the Hall of Perta Vin-Grahl. Mika was with a vampiress, but Larten paid little attention to her. He wanted to congratulate Mika on his recent dealings with the vampaneze. There had been skirmishes between the two clans. Both felt that certain individuals on the other side were acting provocatively. (Larten was fairly sure that Wester was one of the vampires hell-bent on causing trouble, but they rarely discussed such matters.) The centuries-old truce was in danger of crumbling. If it fell, the result would be chaos.

Vancha had been sent to parlay with the vampaneze, and Mika had gone with him. The young, ambitious vampire had been working hard while Larten was away, and had built up a fine reputation for himself. He'd come of age in the tense negotiations. He had suggested some changes to the terms of the truce and helped calm a few of the more agitated vampaneze. Peace had been secured and Vancha made it clear that it was largely thanks to the work of Mika Ver Leth. Wester wasn't pleased – he hungered for war – but most vampires were relieved and Mika was something of a celebrity now.

"Mika!" Larten called, catching up with the dark-haired, steel-eyed General. "Congratulations. I heard about your dealings with the vampaneze. Vancha said you are a born politician."

"I think Sire March gives me undue credit so that those who wanted war turn on me instead of him," Mika snorted. "You, on the other hand, found Perta Vin-Grahl's palace all by yourself. I'm jealous. I plan to travel there in the near future, gods willing, but it won't be the same as being first inside."

Several vampires had already made a pilgrimage to the icy palace, following Larten's directions. A limit had been set on how many could go there in any year – they didn't want to alert the humans who lived in Greenland – but Larten was sure Mika wouldn't have to wait long, given his current status.

"Will you come with me to the Hall named in Perta's honor and tell me about your discovery while I wash?" Mika asked.

"Of course," Larten said. As he fell in line beside Mika, his gaze flicked to the woman walking beside them. Then he stopped and looked hard.

"It took you long enough to notice," the woman sniffed.

"I know you," Larten said as Mika stared at them.

"I should hope so," she said drily. They reached the door of the cavern and went in. The woman undressed and so did Mika. Vampires didn't worry about nudity. There weren't many women in the clan, but those who had been accepted by the gruff Generals were treated the same as the men. They fought together, ate together and bathed together. It was their way, and Larten normally wouldn't have spared the woman a second glance, naked or otherwise.

But he knew her. He couldn't remember from where, but they'd met before, he was sure of it. And there was something about the meeting...something out of the ordinary....

Larten stood by the edge of the pool, fully clothed, gaping at the woman as she washed herself in the chilly spray of the mountain waterfall, trying to recall her name or where he'd last seen her.

"Can't you remember?" she laughed, stepping clear of the natural shower. Mika was squinting at him and Larten had an idea that the high-flying General was fond of his partner and didn't like the way Larten was looking at her.

"Did we meet in Paris?" Larten guessed, though he knew that was wrong. Their meeting went back farther than that.

"I'll give you a clue," the woman said, wringing water from her long dark hair. "You made up a song about me once when you were drunk. You claimed I was nectar to all males and you wanted to hook me like a whale."

"Did he indeed?" Mika thundered.

Larten ignored the indignant General. He recognized her now. He should have known who she was the second he saw her, but a lot had happened since he'd first met the Lady of the Wilds and her sharp-tongued assistant.

"*Arra?*" he gasped, stepping into the water, such was his shock. "*Arra Sails?* What in the name of all the gods are *you* doing here?"

"Washing," she said briskly. "Do you want to scrub my back with a flannel?" When he blushed, Arra laughed at him as merrily as her mistress Evanna once had many years before.

140

Chapter Fourteen

That last month before Council was a distracting time for Larten. He should have been concentrating on his duties, working with his team to get everything in place for the Festival of the Undead. But he kept thinking about Arra Sails, Evanna's onetime apprentice.

Arra spent most of her time with Mika. He wasn't the one who had blooded her, but he'd taken her on as an assistant a couple of years earlier when her original master decided she was too lively for him. It was hard for Larten to catch Arra by herself, but when Mika's back was turned he'd managed to sneak in a few late-night conversations and had learned something of her life since she'd parted ways with the witch.

Larten's stories about the clan had convinced Arra that the vampire way was for her. She had set out in search of a suitable master and finally found one. He was past his prime, but had fought many times and could teach her much. She enjoyed her apprenticeship, but they quarreled with each other a lot. He had been hoping for an assistant to support him in his old age and take care of him.

"The damn fool wanted someone to massage his feet, not back him up in battle," she snorted.

Arra wasn't the quiet, caring assistant the elderly vampire had hoped for. She pushed him hard, tried to reignite the fire in his stomach, urged him to fight often so that she could join him in action and learn. In the end he was relieved when Mika took her off his hands. He hadn't come to Council—he was afraid Mika might foist her back on him!

It was clear to Larten that Arra suffered none of the doubts that had plagued him during his wilderness years. She loved being a vampire, had taken to the life immediately, and was determined to push ahead as fast as she could. She'd already passed more tests than he had at her stage, and hoped to become a

General in five or six years, one of only a very few women to ever hold the rank.

Larten tried to give Arra little gifts in the run-up to Council, to sweeten her, but she rejected them. She didn't want favors or special treatment. She was here to train and fight, not be buttered up by orange-haired charmers.

With no other choice, Larten focused on his job. But it was difficult. This was the first time since Alicia cut him out of her life that he'd shown any interest in another woman. There'd been a spark between him and Arra all those years ago – or so he thought – and he was keen to fan it to life again. But he had never tried to seduce a vampiress before, and he found her a hard nut to crack.

The Festival of the Undead couldn't come quickly enough for Larten. If gifts didn't impress Arra, he hoped a display of skill and strength would. He had come a long way since his first disastrous experience of combat in Vampire Mountain, and fancied himself to give a good showing. Maybe he could woo Arra by breaking lots of bones and skulls.

As soon as the Festival kicked off in its usual chaotic manner, Larten searched for Arra and Mika. It took him a while to track either of them down, and when he eventually found the General – resting after a particularly hairy ax duel – Arra was nowhere to be seen. That disappointed Larten, but he wasn't going to miss the opportunity to put Mika in his place. "Come on," he snapped, striding up to the seated General. "I challenge you. Name your weapon of choice."

Mika trained his gaze on Larten, then shook his head and smiled thinly.

"You cannot refuse me," Larten growled. "No vampire can refuse a challenge during the Festival."

"That's true," Mika said. "If you insist, I will fight. But I'd rather not."

"Afraid I will disgrace you in front of Arra?" Larten sneered.

Mika didn't rise to the bait, although the flesh around his throat turned a deep red color. "I respect you, Larten," he said. "You've gone astray in the past, but I admire the way you've fought back. Any other time I would relish a duel with you. It would be an intriguing contest."

"Then fight me," Larten pressed, but again Mika shook his head.

"You only wish to impress Arra," Mika said. "You

144

want to humiliate me in order to win her approval. Is that not so? Please think before you answer."

Larten was about to snap a denial, but at Mika's request he paused, considered his emotions, then nodded reluctantly.

"I hope to mate with the fierce Miss Sails," Mika said. "You obviously wish to win her hand too. But heed this warning—we'll both lose her if we scrap over her like dogs over a bone. Arra has no time for vain preeners."

Mika stood and offered his hand. Larten grinned and shook it. "We'll fight some other night," Mika promised. "As friends."

"Aye," Larten agreed, then went in search of Arra, chuckling at his foolishness, glad that at least one of them had kept his head. Larten might be a General, but he realized after his showdown with the calmer Mika that he still had a lot to learn.

Larten finally found Arra on the bars, a series of connected wooden poles. Each combatant had to try to knock off their opponent, using a staff with rounded ends. Arra had already defeated a handful of Generals and was making quick work of the latest challenger.

She had an eerie sense of balance and moved swiftly from one wooden bar to the next, her staff held loosely but dangerously by her side. She darted towards and away from her hapless foe, confusing and tiring him, before coolly sweeping his feet from beneath him and sending him tumbling to the floor.

"Who's next?" she barked with excitement, eyes alight. She caught Larten's gaze and cocked an eyebrow.

"Why not?" he muttered and stepped up. He took a few seconds to find his feet, then another vampire handed him a staff. He twirled it over his head and narrowed his eyes. Arra danced from one bar to another, but he ignored that and advanced slowly, staff held low, forcing her back. She wasn't to know, but he also had a fine sense of balance and had rarely lost on the bars at previous Councils. Arra was a natural, but Larten was confident he would get the better of her.

Before they could test each other, a burly vampire was catapulted from a nearby ring. He'd been swinging on a rope that had snapped near the top. He roared as he sailed over the heads of alarmed but laughing Generals, then smashed down on the bars, shattering several and bringing the entire system to the ground.

Larten and Arra were thrown clear. As they picked themselves up, the vampire plucked splinters from his cheeks, swore loudly, then raced back to the ring to grab another rope. The General and the assistant stared at each other then burst out laughing.

"You had a lucky escape," Arra taunted him.

"I would have had you on your back in a few more seconds," Larten countered.

"That might have been fun," Arra murmured.

Larten smiled at her, drew closer and tossed aside his staff. As he pushed in for a kiss, Arra raised her own staff and jabbed him back with the rounded tip. He chuckled, sure that she was playing with him, but she jabbed him harder when he tried to press forward again. "No," she said.

"But I thought..." He felt his face flush. "Do you love Mika?"

"Don't be foolish," Arra said. "Of all the vampires here, you're the one I'd set my eye on if I was in the mood for setting. But I won't be sidetracked. I mean to become a General, and I won't let anything get in the way of that. This isn't a time for romantic games. As long as I'm a mere assistant, I'm placing myself off-limits to rogues like you."

"Is that what you think I am?" Larten asked.

"Aye," she said. "But lucky for you, I like rogues." Arra brought her club up and tapped the side of Larten's head. "There will come a night when I'll welcome your advances, but this isn't it. You'll have to show a little patience if you want to win my heart."

"Then I will wait," Larten answered smoothly. In a flash, he grabbed the top of the staff and thrust hard, knocking Arra over.

"Foul move!" she cried furiously.

"I know," Larten chuckled. "Watch out for it next time. I have to go arrange for the bars to be rebuilt. I will face you on them later."

But they didn't fight that night or for the rest of Council, as both got involved in other challenges and they kept missing each other. There were chances in future years, but in the end Larten never sparred with her on the bars. It wasn't that he was afraid of being beaten by a woman—there would have been no shame in losing to a warrior of Arra's caliber. Events just kept getting in their way. It ultimately became a standing joke between them. Arra would claim that destiny was working against the pair, that they were fated never to duel.

Decades later, when Arra was felled in her prime, Larten would spend many nights wishing that he had made more of an effort to face her at least once on her beloved bars. He regretted all the chances he'd spurned, the way he'd avoided her to prolong the joke, only realizing how limited the opportunities had been once they were gone – like Arra – forever.

Chapter Fifteen

Arra remained at Vampire Mountain with Mika for a few years, then moved on with him when he departed. Larten made a variety of approaches to her while she was there, but she turned him down every time. He was almost glad when she left—at least he couldn't go on making a fool of himself if she wasn't around for him to moon over.

Shortly after Mika and Arra had taken their leave, a troubled Vancha March invited Larten to come see him in the Hall of Princes. The scruffy Prince had been left in charge of the throne room again, but Paris was due to return from a short trip, so he wouldn't have to suffer for long. Vancha was slouched on his throne, picking a toenail, but he didn't look as carefree as normal. "Do you remember Arrow?" he asked.

"Of course." Larten had been impressed by the muscular, bald vampire with the tattooed arrows on his scalp, and admired him for having the courage to withdraw from the affairs of the clan and settle down with a human wife.

"I spoke with Patrick Goulder earlier tonight," Vancha said. "He's just returned from a mission. He spotted Arrow in the course of his travels." Vancha scratched the back of his neck. "Arrow's wife, Sarah, was killed by a vampaneze."

"When?" Larten asked, recalling the quiet, pleasant woman who had welcomed them to her house and served up a fine dinner.

"I don't know. But Arrow took it badly. He's been tracking down every vampaneze he can find, challenging and killing them. Patrick said it's like he wants to work his way through the entire clan."

"Wester will be happy if he does," Larten remarked humorlessly.

"Arrow's done nothing wrong," Vancha said. "He's free to challenge as many vampaneze as he likes. He fights fairly and kills them cleanly."

"But you want to stop him regardless," Larten guessed.

Vancha sighed. "He's on a suicide mission. Arrow's a first-rate warrior, but you can't stumble from one challenge to another and last very long. Patrick said he's killed five or six vampaneze, so he's already pushed his luck to its limits. He might well be dead before I reach him, but I want to try to reason with him if it's not too late. He could still be of service to the clan."

"You think he might return to the fold?" Larten was doubtful.

"Why not?" Vancha shrugged. "You did."

Larten now understood why he'd been summoned. "You want me to come with you. You think I can help him, having been through something like this myself."

"That's about the measure of it," Vancha agreed. "You haven't done much as a General. It's time you proved yourself worthy of your appointment."

"When do we leave?" Larten asked simply.

"As soon as Paris returns, which should be within the next couple of nights."

"I will go and prepare immediately."

"Larten," Vancha stopped him. He was leaning

153

forward intently. "You never say much about her, but you loved a human too, didn't you?"

"Aye," Larten said, thinking of Alicia and feeling his insides tighten as they always did when he recalled her expression that last day outside the shed.

"If she'd been murdered, could it have driven you mad, even knowing she was only human and that she would die long before you anyway?" Larten nodded roughly. "Could you have been persuaded by someone like me to abandon your quest for revenge?" Vancha asked.

"I do not know," Larten said honestly. "Even if I could answer that, I am not Arrow. Loss affects each of us differently. You think we will have trouble trying to reason with him?"

"I wish I knew," Vancha said. "I've only ever truly loved the clan. I find it hard to put myself in his position."

"You should consider that a blessing, Sire," Larten said softly, then went to tell Seba and Wester of his impending departure.

Seba was delighted that Larten was getting a chance to test himself beyond the confines of Vampire Mountain, but Wester was downcast. Larten tried to cheer

154

him up with a few mugs of ale in the Hall of Khledon Lurt, but the guard's mood wouldn't lighten. Finally he confessed what was bothering him.

"I need to get out. I've been here a long time and I'm starting to feel caged in. I've no doubt that this is what I want from life – I'm absolutely committed to the clan –but I need a break, like you did when you left."

"That is natural," Larten said.

"I was thinking.... Would Vancha mind if I asked to accompany you?"

"Possibly," Larten said. "This is a delicate business."

"I know that," Wester snapped. "I'm not expecting sport and excitement."

"Guards do well here in Vampire Mountain," Larten went on, "but they often struggle in the field. You might be a hindrance to us."

Wester's face dropped. "You're right," he mumbled. "Forget about it. I'm –"

"–a gullible fool," Larten interrupted, then laughed at Wester's expression. "Of course you can come. You will have to clear it with Vancha first, but I am sure he will be as pleased as I am to include you. It will be the old Crepsley and Flack team again—we cannot fail."

"You really want me to come along?" Wester asked.

"Do not fish for compliments," Larten growled, then sent Wester off to the Hall of Princes to seek Vancha's permission.

Seba was waiting for Larten when he returned to the small cell that he and Wester shared. The quartermaster was sitting on the lid of Larten's coffin— he had finally gotten into the habit of sleeping in one and couldn't remember what he had ever disliked about them in the first place. Seba beamed when he saw his ex-assistant and said, "Has Wester gone to ask Vancha's permission to join you on your trip?"

"You do not miss much," Larten chuckled.

"I might not be your master any longer," Seba said, "but I keep a close eye on the pair of you. I could tell that Wester was anxious to leave. It will be good for him to get out into the world again. At least it will pry him away from his vampaneze-hating allies for a time."

"You worry about that too?" Larten asked, sitting on the coffin beside his old mentor.

"Wester is heading for trouble," Seba said darkly. "But we must all make our own mistakes in life. I hope his do not prove too costly, and that he learns from them and grows, as you grew from yours."

156

Larten smiled at the kind words, then said softly, "You are wrong."

"About what?" Seba frowned.

"Not being our master. I will always think of you as my master. And as my father."

Seba stared at the younger vampire, then turned aside and coughed. Larten thought he saw the older vampire wiping a few tears from his eyes, but he said nothing.

"Damn dust," Seba growled. He considered telling Larten that he had always thought of him as a son, but figured there was no need to get overly sentimental or they might both end up blubbering like babies. Instead he sniffed and reached behind the coffin. "I meant to give these to you when you became a General. I had been keeping them for years. Moths got at the originals and they fell apart when I took them out of their box. I replaced all of the items later, but I was waiting for the right moment to present you with them. This seems as good a time as any."

Larten smiled uncertainly as he took a wrapped packet from Seba. His ancient friend had never given him a gift before and he had no idea what it might be. He tore away the paper and went very still when he saw what lay inside.

"You might not like them," Seba said. "Do not feel that you have to wear them to please me. I just thought they might be to your taste."

"Thank you," Larten said, and now it was his turn to blink away tears.

"Try them on," Seba said. "If they need to be adjusted, let me know. I have become something of an expert tailor over the centuries."

As Seba left, Larten undressed. He cast away his dark trousers, the gray tunic that he'd worn for some years, the dirty undershirt. Then he carefully pulled on a pair of sharp red trousers, a stiff crimson shirt, and last of all a blood-red cloak. There was no mirror in his cell, but Larten could picture how he looked. He twirled and let the cloak sweep through the air around him. He took the end of one hem, pressed it to the scar on his cheek, then let it drop.

He wasn't sure why he had done that – it just seemed appropriate – but he was certain of one thing. These clothes were a sign that he had come of age, and he would wear them, or replacements like them, for the rest of his life. Only death would part him from this covering of beloved red.

Part Four

"your soul will surely find Paradise"

Chapter Sixteen

Vancha used the Stone of Blood to pinpoint Arrow's position. A vampire trained in the ways of the Stone could search for anyone who had touched it and let it absorb some of their blood. It took him only a minute to locate Arrow. Paris would guide them later, when they drew close to their destination—he had a telepathic link to both Vancha and Larten, and could direct them to Arrow's exact location.

The three vampires left shortly after dusk and set a fast pace. They couldn't flit – it wasn't allowed on the way to or from the mountain – but they proceeded as quickly as the ancient laws permitted.

Wester felt awkward to begin with. He was rusty

after his years inside, lagged behind when they hunted, found it hard to relate when they were talking about matters to do with the outside world. But as the nights slipped away behind them, he settled into his stride and became more like he had been in his youth. He would never be as expert a hunter as Larten or Vancha, and he sometimes struggled to match their pace, but he was no burden.

Larten missed his coffin – he had grown fond of it after his initial doubts – but soon adjusted to sleeping rough again. Vancha was delighted to bed down on hard, cold ground. He wanted nothing to do with the comforts that many vampires indulged in, like coffins, hot meals and ale. Give him a rocky floor, raw meat, fresh blood and a running stream, and he was happy.

After a while Larten noticed a red sheen to Vancha's skin. He thought the Prince had a rash and mentioned it to him, but Vancha said (rather gruffly) that he was fine. Larten said no more about it, but paid close attention to Vancha for the next few nights. He soon learned that the Prince rose an hour before sunset every evening and walked around unprotected, letting the rays of the sun scald him. This fascinated Larten. He couldn't understand why the Prince should put himself through such torment. He discussed it with Wester, but the guard could offer no explanation either. They both wanted to ask, but Princes weren't accountable to lesser vampires. If Vancha wished to tell them, he would. Otherwise they would have to go on guessing.

The trio avoided contact with humans, only slipping into towns and villages in the dead of night to feed quietly, then moving on unseen. Larten felt no pangs of regret when they occasionally heard the laughter and singing of people having a good time, or glimpsed them through frost-speckled windows. He had found his true family and was content at last to be only a vampire and nothing more.

The world was at war again, and this battle was more widespread and bloodier than any Larten had seen. Weapons had advanced significantly since he'd last taken to a battlefield, and the cunning, bloodthirsty marshals of the mayhem had managed to cram more of their companions into the firing line than ever before. The slaughter of thousands was no longer enough to satisfy the vicious beast of war. It required hundreds of thousands of victims now, even millions.

Larten wondered where it would end. How much

further could people go in their quest for the perfect weapon, the ultimate annihilation, the kill to end all kills? Winning didn't seem to be an issue anymore. With losses on this scale, there could be no real victor. Success appeared to be calculated in the number of dead enemies, not in material gains.

Vancha and Wester were equally horrified by this new war of trenches, machine guns, poison gas and tanks. They had seen mankind at what they'd thought was its worst. As Cubs, Wester and Larten had feasted in war zones and merrily watched soldiers killing each other. Vampires were coarse creatures, lovers of battle, connoisseurs of combat. But there was no pleasure to be wrung from this wretched, pointless butchery. No young vampires cheered on these warring sides or gambled on their fortunes. There was nothing noble or exciting about this massacre. It was simply a sickening waste of life.

Progress across the war zone was difficult. Vampires were tougher than humans, but they could be killed the same way—they weren't immune to bullets, bombs or gas. Arrow was somewhere in the middle of the madness, so they had to advance carefully, skirting the trenches of doomed soldiers, slipping through fields of corpses in the darkest hours of the night, seeking shelter in craters during the day. All three saw horrors that they hadn't witnessed before, things they'd never speak of later and would try in vain to forget.

One cold, wet night as shells rained around them, Larten heard a noise close by. They were in the middle of what the humans called no-man's-land, a zone of barbed wire, bomb craters and scraps of the dead. Soldiers sometimes made dashes across this expanse of wasteland in the day, to be mown down by the ravenous fire of machine guns, but even their harshest officers weren't heartless enough to send them out here at night.

Larten rolled onto his side, wriggled to the top of the hole in which they were pinned, and peered into the smoke-obscured darkness. For a while he saw nothing and began to think that he had imagined the sound. But as the missiles temporarily ceased, he spotted a group of nine soldiers adrift in the open. Nobody else had seen them yet, but once someone sighted them, they would be exposed to fire from all sides.

The soldiers must have been separated from their regiment, or were survivors of a damned dash across no-man's-land. Most were bleeding from poorly bandaged injuries as they crawled or were dragged by their companions. They didn't seem to have any idea where they were going. They were arguing – quietly, so as not to draw attention – and drifting vaguely. It was only a matter of time before they were pinpointed and killed.

Larten recalled something that Vancha had said, that destiny would probably place him in a situation where he could partly atone for killing the humans on the ship. Larten knew in his heart that this was such a moment. "I am going out," he whispered.

"What are you talking about?" Wester frowned.

"There are soldiers…they have been cut off… they are trying to make their way back to their army."

"So?" Wester shrugged. "Thousands are sacrificed every day. Why risk your life for these few?"

"I can do nothing about the thousands," Larten said softly, "but I can maybe help this group." He stared at Vancha, hoping the Prince would know why he had to try.

"You must follow your instincts," Vancha said. "If helping them will ease your conscience, then do it."

"Nothing will ever ease my conscience," Larten said sadly. "But it is the right thing to do, and I have done the wrong thing too often in the past."

Wester was bewildered—Larten had never told

him about the ship and the people he'd murdered. The guard started to quiz his old friend, but there was no time for explanations. As Vancha made the death's touch sign, Larten slid over the top of the crater and hurried towards the stranded soldiers.

They didn't see him until he was almost upon them. A couple spotted him at the last second and hastily raised their bayonets. He stopped and showed his palms, letting them know that he meant no harm. One snapped a question at him, but Larten only shook his head—if he spoke, they'd know by his accent that he wasn't one of them, and that might cause them to panic.

It took him a few seconds to determine the color of their uniforms – it was dark and they were dusty and bloodied – but when he figured out which side they belonged to, he pointed towards the nearest safe trench. The soldier in charge – he looked too young to be an officer – shook his head and pointed in a different direction. That way would lead them to safety too, but it was a longer route and they'd pass close to their enemies.

Larten hesitated, then stood and let his cloak billow behind him, ignoring the fact that he would be an easy target if any snipers caught sight of him. In his red suit and flapping cloak, with his orange hair and scar, he looked like some sort of warped angel. The soldiers knew instantly that he wasn't one of them. They had heard tales of spirits on the battlefield, kindly ghosts who led stray soldiers back to their ranks, wicked demons who misguided them into a shower of bullets. Most hadn't believed the tales...until now.

Larten could see a mixture of fear and hope in their eyes. They wanted to think that he was one of the good spirits, that they could trust him. But he looked more like a messenger from hell than heaven. And red was the color of the devil.

Larten was exasperated, but he couldn't blame them. In their muddy, bloody boots, with so much at stake, he might have faltered too. Looking from one to another, he isolated the soldier in the worst condition. He was missing his lower left leg and his upper body had been pierced by shrapnel in many places. Larten stepped forward, brushed past the raised bayonets and picked up the wounded man. He settled him on his shoulders like a lamb, then set off through the wire, corpses and darkness. If the others followed, he would guide them. If not, at least he had tried.

When he heard the rest of the group scrabbling

after him, Larten smiled tightly and bent lower, trying not to appear as so much of a target if any of the soldiers in the trenches spotted him.

He felt the man on his back shudder then stiffen on their way to the trench. He knew that life had passed from the young soldier, but he didn't pause or set him down. *I will make a deal with you*, Larten said silently to the spirit of the dead man. *If you protect us from the guns and grenades, I will carry you all the way to your people and ensure that you are not buried in a nameless grave.*

Maybe the soldier heard and hid them from the gaze of their foes, or perhaps it was only the luck of the vampires, but Larten made it to the trench in one piece and the others toppled in behind him. Some were giggling hysterically as they slid out of the line of fire. All were gaping at the figure in the red cloak. A couple crossed themselves.

Saying nothing, Larten set down the dead soldier. One of the man's eyes was open. Larten closed it, then made the death's touch sign and silently repeated the ancient words that vampires had said over their dead for time immemorial.

Then, before the soldiers could challenge him, Larten swept out of the trench and retraced his steps through no-man's-land. He didn't congratulate himself as he wound his way back to Wester and Vancha. Nothing could ever truly atone for his crimes on the ship. A life saved couldn't cancel out a murder.

But in that land of chaos, that time of blood-drenched madness, Larten had done a decent thing. In the end that would have to be enough, because no matter how long he lived or where his path took him, that was the best he would ever be able to do.

It was probably a foolish fancy, but for a shadow of a second Larten thought he sensed the shade of a young girl behind him. She had been called Malora when she was alive, but he didn't know if the dead had any use for names. He imagined her hovering in the darkness, a spirit of the battlefield. And he thought…he *hoped* she was watching him with a slight but heartfelt flicker of an approving smile.

Chapter Seventeen

They found Arrow in the remains of a mansion. It had been bombed earlier in the war. Now the troops had moved on and the area was eerily peaceful. It felt like the graveyard where Larten had first run into Seba, the scorched earth dark and alien beneath a quarter-full moon, just a scattering of grass and weeds, hints that the land would one day recover from even this brutal treatment.

Arrow was sitting on a log in the middle of what must once have been a grand dining room. Now there was no glass in the windows, the walls were black with soot, half the ceiling had fallen in, and there were old bloodstains on the floor.

"I didn't expect you to come with support," Arrow said as the trio of vampires slid into the room. He was sitting with his back to them and there was scorn in his voice. "Were you afraid to face me on your own?"

"Why should I be afraid of a friend?" Vancha asked.

Arrow spun with shock, his eyes widening. He looked much the same as when Larten had last seen him, except he had a scraggly beard and his eyes were dark with horror and hatred. "Vancha!" he gasped, lurching to his feet. "And... Larten, isn't it?"

"Aye," Larten nodded.

"And that's Wester Flack," Vancha said cheerily. "I assume by your reaction that you were expecting somebody else?"

"Yes. I never..." The large vampire frowned, the tattoos of arrows on the sides of his head crinkling. "What are you doing here? It can't be coincidence."

"Of course it isn't," Vancha chuckled. "We heard about your quest to single-handedly rid the world of vampaneze and we–"

"–came to help me, I hope," Arrow growled. "Or do you plan to stand in my way? That had better not be the case. We're old friends, Vancha, but don't assume that I won't strike you down like one of the purple scum if you try to stop me."

"That's Sire Vancha, actually," Vancha said.

"What are you talking about?"

"I'm a Prince now."

Arrow blinked, then smiled thinly. "Congratulations. I mean that, even if I can't muster the enthusiasm to make it sound genuine. The clan chose well. I'm sure you'll serve admirably."

"Larten's had an eventful few years too," Vancha said, the artless signal for the General to try to reason with Arrow.

"I fell in love with a human," Larten said. "I asked her to marry me. I thought I could be happy with her, as you were with Sarah."

Arrow's face softened at the mention of his dead wife's name. He relaxed, sat on the log again and said to Larten, "Did she accept your offer of marriage?"

"Aye."

"Then why are you here?"

Larten grimaced. "I told her many things about myself when I was wooing her, but I forgot to tell her that I was a vampire."

"A strange oversight," Arrow remarked drily.

"I was going through a bad time," Larten said

softly. "I did not want to be a night-walker. I hid from myself and she fell in love with the man I was pretending to be. For a while we were happy. But when the truth came out..."

"She banished you?" Arrow guessed.

Larten nodded. "If I had told her to begin with, maybe things would have been different. But nothing good can come of lies. A lie will always come back to haunt a person in the end."

"You speak wisely," Arrow said, then cackled bitterly. "But your loss – and if I'm any judge, that's why Vancha brought you – is nothing like mine. I was always honest with Sarah. She didn't cast me aside for being a vampire. She accepted me for what I was. But I lost her anyway. She was murdered."

"Can you tell us about it?" Larten asked. "We do not know much, only that she was killed. Did a vampaneze feed from her?"

"I would have roasted in the fires of a dozen hells before I'd have ever let that happen," Arrow snarled. "The vampaneze aren't fools. They drink carefully, never from a human who has anything to do with vampires. They fear war as much as the clan does, as much as *I* once did."

"You don't fear it any longer?" Wester asked.

176

"I'd welcome it with open arms," Arrow said darkly.

Larten shot Wester a dirty look – *Keep quiet!* – then focused on Arrow again as the heartbroken loner told his story. He and Sarah had adopted a few children, as they had said they would when Larten and Vancha last saw them. They reared the children and lived happily. Arrow sometimes felt sad when he watched Sarah grow older, but she was healthy and he hoped they'd have maybe another twenty or thirty years together before death parted them.

Then a vampaneze found Arrow by chance. He was young, in search of glory. He challenged Arrow to a duel, but the vampire refused. The vampaneze persisted. Arrow rebuffed him, hoping he'd lose interest and move on, but the young warrior came one night and grabbed Sarah. He threatened to kill her if Arrow didn't fight.

Having no choice, Arrow met the vampaneze's challenge and they dueled in front of the cottage where he, Sarah and their adopted children had lived for so many years. Sarah watched with terror, praying for her husband to survive.

Arrow hadn't fought for a long time, but he was stronger and faster than the vampaneze. It soon became clear that he had the better of his brash challenger.

When Arrow knocked him down for the fifth or sixth time, the vampaneze lay stunned and bleeding in the grass. All Arrow had to do was bend over and finish him off. But Sarah had no taste for blood. As Arrow advanced, she cried out to him to be merciful.

"I should have known better," Arrow croaked, trembling with rage and self-hatred. "Vampires and vampaneze don't give any quarter when they fight. Mercy is a human conceit. If I hadn't been apart from the clan for so long, I would have killed him cleanly, the way any true warrior deserves."

But Arrow didn't want to act like a brutal beast in front of the woman he loved. His years spent living as a human had clouded his judgment and led him to think and reason as one of them. With a heavy sigh, he spared the vampaneze's life and told him to leave. He forgot that a vampaneze would rather die in agony than live in disgrace, that mercy would be misinterpreted as an insult by any member of the night clans.

As Arrow took a few breaths to steady himself, the vampaneze rose, slid a knife from his belt and threw it. But not at Arrow — at Sarah. It struck her in the middle of her throat and she collapsed with a soft *whumph.*

"*Whumph,*" Arrow repeated, sounding it carefully, as if it were a precious word.

Arrow screamed her name and rushed to her, but it was too late. Her lips moved as she lay dying in his arms, but she couldn't say anything. She died with her eyes open, staring at the clouds.

When Arrow finally set her aside and turned – he didn't know if it was five minutes or five hours later – the vampaneze was standing behind him, sneering.

"Kill me now, fool," the vampaneze jeered.

And Arrow did.

"But it wasn't enough," he finished. A hard edge had crept into his voice. "Sarah was worth ten of his foul kind. Fifty. A hundred. More. I won't stop until her death has been paid for in full."

"How many will it take?" Vancha asked quietly.

"*All,*" Arrow croaked. Then he smiled savagely. "And here comes the next. Perfect timing."

Arrow rose and the others glanced over their shoulders. A vampaneze was standing by the open window. Larten had no idea how long he'd been there or how much of Arrow's story he had heard. But by the nervous look in his eyes, Larten imagined he'd learned more than he cared to.

"You challenged me last night," the vampaneze said stiffly.

"Aye," Arrow sniffed.

"It was not the right time or place for a fight—"

"So you said."

"—but I have come to face you now, as I vowed."

"I won't keep you waiting any longer," Arrow said and headed for the door.

"Should we try to stop this?" Larten asked quietly.

"No," Vancha sighed. "We must let them fight."

The three vampires followed Arrow out to where the vampaneze was waiting. As the pair faced each other, no weapons other than their hands, the vampaneze said, "I know that you are Arrow of the vampire clan. Would you have my name before we fight?"

Arrow shook his head. "I don't care for it. Your kind aren't worthy of names. If I kill you, I'll think of you only as number nine."

"As you wish," the vampaneze said coldly.

They clashed.

It was a short, brutal battle. To any watching human it would have appeared as a blur, but Larten could follow the action with his heightened senses.

The pair tore at each other with their fingers, nails sharper than knives. The vampaneze almost slit open one of Arrow's eyes, but just missed and scraped his skull instead. Arrow in return nicked the flesh beneath the vampaneze's throat.

They clutched each other and wrestled furiously. The vampaneze nearly threw Arrow to the ground, but the vampire managed to keep his balance. Wrapping an arm around his foe's head, Arrow tried to snap his neck, but the vampaneze dug his chin down and bit into Arrow's hand.

They broke, panting. A moment's pause, then they hurled themselves into attack again. The vampaneze straightened the fingers of his right hand and jabbed them at Arrow's stomach. The vampire twisted out of the way, but the makeshift blade stabbed into his side and stuck. He roared with pain, but instead of pulling clear, he rolled closer, trapping the vampaneze's hand in his flesh and bending it back.

The vampaneze's wrist snapped and he screamed. He tried to push Arrow away, but the vampire grabbed hold of his foe's good hand and pinned it to his side. He made a fist of his free fingers and smashed it into the vampaneze's throat.

The vampaneze's red eyes widened and his purple

face turned a darker color as he gasped for air. Arrow punched his doomed opponent's throat again, crushing it completely. Then he pried out the hand embedded in his side and shoved the stricken vampaneze away, leaving him to fall, thrash weakly and die.

Vancha stepped forward as Arrow was examining his wounds. Crouching by the dying vampaneze, he made the death's touch sign by placing his middle finger on his forehead, the fingers beside that over his eyes, and stretching out his thumb and little finger. "Even in death may you be triumphant," he whispered.

When the vampaneze fell still, Vancha confronted Arrow. "You should have accepted his name," the Prince growled. "He faced you openly and died bravely. He deserved to be remembered."

"Drink his blood if he matters that much to you," Arrow sneered. Vampires could retain the memories of humans if they drained them of blood.

"You know that we cannot drink the blood of a vampaneze," Vancha said.

Arrow shrugged sarcastically.

Vancha exchanged an uncertain look with Larten. They had come here to try to make the renegade vampire see reason, but the Prince could think of nothing

182

to say. Larten didn't believe that he could help Arrow either, but he steeled himself to try. He planned to ask Arrow what Sarah would have thought of such barbarism. He hoped that guilt would make Arrow pause and see sense.

But before Larten could say anything, Wester said softly, "This is wrong."

Arrow cocked a bitter eyebrow. "You pity the vampaneze?"

"No."

"You think there was anything unlawful about the way I fought?"

"No."

"Then what was wrong about it?" Arrow growled.

"You can't kill them all by yourself," Wester said.

Arrow frowned. That wasn't what he had expected.

Wester knelt by the dead vampaneze, dipped three fingers into the blood that was pooling around the corpse's body, and smeared it across his own left cheek, making marks similar to those that the vampaneze scratched on their human victims before they killed them. He dipped his fingers in the blood again and faced Arrow.

"Others hate the vampaneze as much as you do," Wester said. "They're traitors to the clan, foul killers, worthless scum. They must be destroyed and forgotten."

Wester stepped closer to the startled, almost hypnotized Arrow. "You waste your time and energy fighting them alone. Come back with us. Train to become a General. Join those who feel as you do and help us. Only a war can ease your pain and satisfy the demands of your lost, dead love."

"The vampires will never go to war with the vampaneze," Arrow mumbled.

"They will," Wester contradicted him. "If enough of us seek it, the Princes will listen. If we recruit vampires of influence and respect – as you once were and can be again – we'll bend the clan to our will. It probably won't happen soon, but there *will* come a time of reckoning. I swear it on this blood."

Wester reached out and wiped his fingers across Arrow's cheek. Arrow flinched and almost withdrew, but then stood firm and accepted the mark, laying his hand over Wester's and squeezing firmly. Larten and Vancha were disturbed by the grisly nature of the dark pact, but neither interrupted. They just stood, watching numbly, troubled by Wester's prediction, wondering if this was the grim, vengeful face of things to come.

Chapter Eighteen

Later, away from the scene of the challenge, Vancha and Larten sat apart from Wester and Arrow. Wester was telling Arrow about those who hated the vampaneze and the steps they were taking to win others over to their cause. Arrow was listening intently. The pair barely noticed when their allies retreated to hold their own hushed council.

"I don't like this," Vancha muttered, stroking the tips of his shurikens as if for comfort. "Vampires of good standing don't scheme and talk of mass elimination. It isn't our way."

"But you must have known that this was building," Larten said. "Wester and his companions have been plotting the downfall of the vampaneze for decades. This cannot be news to you."

"No," Vancha said. "But I hadn't given the matter much consideration until tonight. I never realized feelings ran this deeply."

"Well, evidently they do," Larten said. "What can we do about it?"

Vancha sighed. "Not much, I suppose. As long as they don't openly criticize the Princes, we can't punish them for plotting. Every vampire is free to believe as he pleases. We expect members of the clan to respect our decisions, but we don't ask them to accept our judgments without question. As long as Wester and his kind don't undermine our command, we must leave them be. We can try to reason with them, but I doubt we'll enjoy much success, not if that pair are anything to go by."

"What if they gather more support?" Larten asked. "If members of their group get invested as Princes, they could lead us to war."

"I think we're a long way from that," Vancha said, but he looked doubtful.

"Maybe we should leave Arrow behind," Larten suggested. "The clan might be better off without him."

Vancha shook his head. "We can't hide from our

186

fears. If we don't openly engage with the likes of Arrow and Wester, they'll scheme in secret, and that will be even worse. I don't think this is the true Arrow—he's still grieving, in shock after Sarah's death. I believe I can draw him back to his senses over the coming months, turn him from the path of hatred."

"But if you cannot?" Larten asked.

Vancha shrugged. "We'll deal with that later if we have to." Vancha was silent for a long time. When he spoke again, he surprised Larten. "You're not coming back to Vampire Mountain, are you?"

"How did you know?" Larten gasped.

Vancha chuckled. "You can always read a man's intentions in his eyes. I've seen your gaze stray to the horizon in recent nights."

Larten nodded. "There are some people I wish to check on. They live – or lived – not far from here, so it should not take long. Of course, I will come with you if you prefer."

"No," Vancha said. "You're a General now. You can come and go as you please. I brought you along to reason with Arrow, but I don't think he'll listen in his current state. Your mission is at an end. See to your other business." Vancha glanced at Wester and

Arrow then lowered his voice. "Will you invite Wester to travel with you? I'd like to separate him from Arrow. If we're lucky, by the time they meet again, Arrow might no longer be interested in what Wester has to say."

Larten hesitated. He hadn't liked what he'd seen of Wester tonight and he felt strangely nervous. They had traveled together since they were youths and shared everything. Apart from Seba, he was closer to Wester than anyone. Yet he felt now as if he didn't truly know the man he thought of as a brother. Larten was half afraid that Wester would weave a spell and turn him into a rabid, vampaneze-hating zealot.

As soon as that ridiculous thought crossed his mind, Larten dismissed it. "I will gladly invite Wester to travel with me," he told Vancha. "He might not choose to come, but if he does, I will welcome his company."

"Well said," Vancha smiled and they returned to sit with the conspirators — their friends.

Wester was happy to travel on with Larten. He wasn't ready to return to Vampire Mountain and didn't feel like he needed to babysit Arrow. He had planted his seed in Arrow's mind and was confident that it would grow over the coming years. Vampires were more patient than humans. Change rarely happened quickly in their world. Wester was in no rush to lead the clan into war. He believed it would happen in its own good time and he didn't mind waiting.

Arrow wasn't so sure about his direction. He had parted ways with the clan when he'd married a human and thought he might not be welcomed back. Vancha told him that some would undoubtedly hold him in low esteem, and he'd have to work hard to prove himself again. But if he was true and brave, he would be accepted.

As the Prince and Arrow circled the trenches and warring humans, Larten headed deeper into the heart of the conflict. His ultimate destination lay beyond the ranks of soldiers, but he had a stop to make first. He'd sensed the witch's presence a few weeks earlier, a tickle at the back of his mind. He wasn't sure if she'd greet him warmly or carve open his other cheek and kill him, but Evanna was in the vicinity and it was time he faced her again.

Larten didn't talk much with Wester while they made their way through the war-ravaged land. Partly this was because they had to concentrate to stay alive and there wasn't time for long conversations. But mostly he didn't know what to say. He still loved his blood brother, but he feared what Wester was becoming. Larten had no doubts that a war with the vampaneze would be catastrophic. The two night clans had held the peace for hundreds of years. There was room enough in this world for both of them. War was the last thing anyone should wish for.

But he knew he couldn't convince Wester to reconsider, just as Wester knew he couldn't persuade Larten to join his cause. It was better, Larten figured, that they say nothing to each other for a while. He still didn't think that Wester and his group could find enough supporters to change the position of the Princes. If Larten ignored Wester's crazy campaign, he hoped it would eventually run out of steam and fade away to nothing. For the sake of the clan, he prayed that it would.

A few nights later, the pair came to a tent in the middle of no-man's-land. It was in plain sight of the trenches of both armies, but no soldier fired on them as they approached and no shells were launched at the tent. The humans might not be familiar with the infamous Lady of the Wilds, but she could cast her spell over them as surely as over any vampire or vampaneze.

Larten hesitated as he drew close, wondering how to announce himself. He was at the point of losing his nerve and retreating when the flap of the tent was thrown back and Evanna stepped out, hands on her hips, ugly as ever, clad in the ropes she almost always wore. "Larten Crepsley," she purred dangerously, eyes narrow. "Or is it Vur Horston or Quicksilver these times?"

"Larten," he said, dropping to one knee. It didn't surprise him that she knew about his other names. Evanna's powers were legendary.

"And Wester Flack," Evanna said, smiling thinly. "Have you come to court me too? Do you think you can succeed where this one failed?"

"Lady?" Wester blinked. Larten had never told him how he came by his scar.

"I do not come to court you," Larten said humbly. "Merely to apologize."

Evanna glared at him, then laughed warmly. "You don't need to say sorry. If anything, *I* should beg pardon for overreacting."

"You were entirely justified," Larten said.

"Maybe, maybe not," Evanna sniffed. "Why don't we discuss it inside, where it's warmer?" And she held the flap open and gestured for them to enter. As Larten passed, she stroked his scar softly with a finger, then shuffled in after him, firmly closing the flap on the world and the war outside.

Chapter Nineteen

Evanna laid out a feast for the hungry vampires. There was no meat or fish but the vegetables were delicious and the pair tucked in heartily. Afterwards they filled her in on all the latest clan-related news. Larten suspected that the witch already knew most of what they told her, but she listened politely and reacted with what seemed like genuine surprise when they talked about Vancha becoming a Prince and Arrow returning to the fold.

"It's been a long time since Arrow came to visit me," she purred. "I always thought he was one of the more charming vampires. Does he still have that deep, smoldering gaze?"

Larten and Wester looked at each other blankly. They'd never noticed a *deep, smoldering gaze* in any man. Evanna laughed and passed them another dish.

"What about your other friends?" she asked Wester. "Are they as determined as ever to bring down the dreaded vampaneze?"

"We aren't afraid of them, Lady," Wester said stiffly. "We just hate them."

Evanna smiled icily. Larten was reminded of an impression he'd formed when they'd first met, that the Lady of the Wilds didn't actually like Wester Flack.

"In my experience," Evanna said, "those who hate are doomed to become slaves to their hatred. It consumes them like a disease, but it is an illness they cannot – or do not want to – live without. Tell me, Wester, if you kill all of the vampaneze, who will you hate then?"

Wester frowned. "Nobody."

"No?" Evanna widened her eyes. "Then what will give your life purpose?"

"I don't understand what you mean," Wester snapped.

Evanna waved it away. "Hopefully you'll never find out. If destiny is gracious, the tribes of the night will settle their differences and put the ways of hatred and war behind them forever."

Larten leaned forward. He had a hidden reason for visiting Evanna and this seemed like the perfect moment to raise it. (He would think later that perhaps she had mentioned destiny in order to give him the excuse to speak.) "I found the tomb of Perta Vin-Grahl some years ago," he said.

"That must have been exciting," Evanna replied lightly, and Larten was sure she already knew that he'd discovered it and what he was going to say next.

"I met your father there," Larten went on, not mentioning the fact that Mr. Tiny had saved him from suicide—he didn't want to tell Wester how close he had come to ending it all.

"Desmond has a habit of cropping up in the strangest of places," Evanna said.

"I was…in trouble." He chose his words with care. "I almost fell into a chasm. He saved me."

"You never told me about that," Wester said, staring at Larten.

Larten shrugged without glancing away from Evanna. "I wondered if you knew why he pulled me back when it would have been easier to let me perish."

Evanna tugged at one of her pointed ears. Her miscolored eyes were cloudy. "My father and I see certain facets of the future," she murmured. "He sees more than I do, and can influence the dice of destiny in ways that I cannot. But the future is rarely set in stone. Many paths twist into it from the present and it isn't always possible to tell which an individual will tread."

"But you have an idea in my case." Larten didn't phrase it as a question.

"I might," she said grudgingly. "But I can't share that insight with you. I am bound by laws that exceed all others. And you wouldn't want to know, even if I were free to tell you. Who wishes to be made aware in advance of the manner or hour of their death?"

"I wouldn't mind," Wester chuckled. "I could hold my wake before I died." But he was ignored. Neither Larten nor Evanna was in the mood for jokes.

"Can you tell me *anything*?" Larten pressed. "I would not ask under other circumstances, but the meddling of Desmond Tiny worries me. He is known for his interference and cruelty. He plays with people, twists their lives and wrings foul pleasure from their torment. If he has such plans for me, I wish to know, so that I can at least mount a fair fight."

Evanna glanced aside. "You shouldn't criticize my father in front of me," she said sullenly.

"Truth is not a criticism," Larten replied. "I said nothing about him that is not true."

Evanna scowled then straightened. "I'll tell you this and no more. If you die the way I suspect – and that's by no means guaranteed – you'll die having led a good life in service to the clan and content that your death has made a difference. It will be a noble end and your soul will surely find Paradise."

"Paradise!" Larten gasped. He had long given up on the possibility of going to Paradise when his soul passed on.

"You shouldn't be surprised," Evanna said. "You've made mistakes and you'll make more if you live long enough. But you have tried to put them right. If you continue to do that, you'll be able to hold your head up proudly when your hour comes, and I don't believe any higher force will deny you the reward that awaits beyond.

"Now enough of such ponderous matters," she said with a smile. "Tell me about my old assistant Arra and how she's faring among the chauvinistic warriors of the clan."

They spent the day in Evanna's tent, resting in comfort. Several humans came to visit her. The soldiers seemed to wander in by accident, but Larten was sure they had been summoned. Evanna greeted each man differently and with a variety of faces. She could change shape and did so many times, depending on her visitor. Larten didn't know if these were men doomed to die, whom she wished to comfort, or soldiers she hoped to influence, to help bring the dirty war to an end.

At dusk, as they prepared to take their leave, Evanna gave Larten a set of flat metal discs. He studied them uncertainly. Evanna smirked and pressed the middle of one. At her touch it sprung into the shape of a small pan. "I know how difficult it is to cook without pots or pans," she said. "You can't carry normal kitchenware when you travel, but these will fit neatly into any bag or sack. Consider them repayment for the scar that I inflicted on you."

"There was no need for this," Larten said. "But I accept your gift with heartfelt thanks."

Evanna smiled and took hold of Larten's chin, tilting his head back so that she could study the scar. She was wearing her regular face, ugly and withered, but Larten thought she was beautiful. He couldn't resist whispering, "If you get lonely any night soon, I could return and keep you company."

Evanna laughed and tweaked his chin. "I see why you caught Arra's eye, you cunning lothario. And poor Malora's too."

It was the first time she'd mentioned her other assistant. Larten's smile faded and he thought for a moment that Evanna was blaming him. When she saw what he was thinking, she shook her head briskly. "That wasn't your fault. It was her destiny. Malora had a touch of foresight—that's why I chose her to serve me. She could have been a powerful sorceress if she'd completed her training, but that was not her wish. She had a feeling her time would be short if she went with you, but she didn't care. You were the one she wanted and I think the months she spent by your side meant more to her than any of the years she might have otherwise lived."

Larten blinked back tears. "Will my life always be this dark and twisted?" he croaked. "Is it my destiny to forever cross paths with the damned or hurt those who would have been better off without me?"

"Only time will tell," Evanna said. "But remember this, Larten—the damned can sometimes be saved. And it is better to be hurt by one you love than never know love at all. You're a better man than you think and many would consider this world a lesser place without you. I am one of them."

Then, to Larten's astonishment, Evanna stood on her tiptoes and kissed his scar. As he gaped, she giggled and threw him out of her tent. He sailed through the air and landed in a heap several feet away. By the time he recovered, the flap had snapped shut. He and Wester had been dismissed.

"She's a strange fish," Wester remarked drily.

"Weird but wonderful," Larten agreed. A soldier passed them, eyes unfocused, heading for reasons he couldn't comprehend to the tent in the middle of no-man's-land.

"Where next?" Wester asked, looking around edgily—he wasn't sure that they were protected any longer.

"Paris," Larten said softly.

"To see the Eiffel Tower?" Wester beamed.

"No," Larten sighed. "To try to find a woman I once loved."

Part Five

*"let your hand rise or fall as destiny
decides it must"*

Chapter Twenty

Alicia no longer lived in the apartment that they had once shared. That didn't surprise Larten, since he had been gone for more than a decade. He wasn't even sure she still lived in the city—she wasn't a native and might have moved since he'd last seen her. Maybe she fled Europe like so many others when the war began. But Larten doubted it. Alicia wasn't the sort to run away from a problem.

The city had changed dramatically and the horrors of the war were reflected in the eyes of the people on the streets. Paris no longer felt like a gay, bubbly city, but a place where death had set up shop.

Larten spent a couple of nights hanging around

the old neighborhood, hoping to spot Alicia or one of her friends. When that failed, he visited the casinos he had once frequented with Tanish Eul.

Some of the casinos had closed down, but others were going strong under new management. Soldiers thronged to the dimly lit rooms at night, eager to enjoy themselves before heading for the trenches and most probably death. Money was gambled recklessly. Women flitted from one desperate man to another. They were lonely, pitiful places and Larten wondered how he'd ever felt at home in dens like these.

While most of the people in the casinos were strangers to him, there were a few familiar faces, croupiers, waiters, some of Tanish's *pretty things*. Larten was sure they'd remember him – his orange crop of hair and long scar marked him in the memories of most people – and that was a worry. He had left Paris having been framed for murder. If he was recognized, it would mean trouble. So he hid behind a cap and scarf whenever he went out, and let Wester do all the talking.

Wester spread a story that Larten was a friend of one of Alicia's relatives and had been given a valuable keepsake to pass to her when the man was killed in battle. He also said that Larten had been wounded in the trenches and was covering his injuries, which was why he never showed his face. There were lots of men in that sad position, so nobody had reason to doubt him.

It took them a long time to find anyone who knew of Alicia – she'd never had much to do with Tanish's business associates – but finally they received word that she was living in the suburbs, where she had moved with her husband and child.

When Larten heard that Alicia had married, he felt both jealousy and delight. A selfish part of him had hoped she'd mourn for him the rest of her life. But mostly he was happy that she'd found someone who could give her all that he had failed to provide. He almost departed Paris when he heard that she had settled down and started a family, but he wanted to make sure that all was well with her and Gavner before he went. He had no intention of letting them see him. He planned to observe them from afar, satisfy himself that they were content, then slip out of their lives forever.

They hadn't been given an exact address, but it was easy enough to track down Alicia once they located the suburb. Wester went from shop to shop, asking about her. He said nothing of a keepsake now,

207

in case she heard and grew wary. He just claimed to be an old friend who was passing through.

When they found out where Alicia was living, they made camp that evening on the roof opposite her building. Larten hadn't said much since they came to Paris. He trembled as they waited, excited and nervous at the thought of seeing his old love again.

Larten stiffened each time the door to the building opened, but it was never Alicia. As the sun rose the next morning, they covered themselves with a sheet of dark felt – Wester had thought ahead – and put on sunglasses to protect their sensitive eyes. Wester never suggested that they leave and return when it was dark. He knew Larten wouldn't retreat until he'd seen Alicia. If that meant a week-long, uncomfortable wait, so be it. Wester would have endured a lot worse than that to assist his blood brother.

Finally, early in the afternoon, the door opened and this time Larten gave a soft moan. Wester raised his sunglasses and squinted. The woman had long, light red hair, a good figure and a beautiful face. She was dressed fashionably and smiled as she strolled down the street, nodding to her neighbors. There was a young girl with her, no more than three years old. She tottered along on short, chubby legs and the woman held her hand and walked slowly, encouraging her.

Wester sneaked a look at Larten. He wasn't crying, but his lips were a thin line and he was shaking softly. The regret in Larten's eyes made Wester look away. He didn't say anything until half an hour later, when the woman and girl returned and went back inside the building, the girl clutching a small bag of sticky sweets.

"She looks happy," Wester said, hoping that was what Larten wished to hear.

"Aye," Larten sighed, but he wasn't so sure. He knew Alicia intimately and had noted a shadow in her expression.

"Do you think the girl is hers?" Wester asked.

"I am sure of it. She has her mother's face."

Wester waited. When Larten gave no sign that he was thinking about moving, Wester cleared his throat. "Have you seen enough?"

"Go if you want to," Larten snapped.

"I'm in no hurry. I'll stay as long as you like. But I thought all you wanted was to make sure that she was all right. You've seen that she is, so why linger?"

"Gavner," Larten muttered. "I want to see him too."

"The boy?" Wester frowned. "What age is he now?"

Larten considered that. He had been thinking of Gavner as he'd last seen him, but of course the child would have grown. "He must be a young man," Larten said wonderingly.

"Then he probably isn't living with them," Wester said.

"He might be," Larten disagreed. "Humans do not marry and move out of their homes as early as they once did."

Wester hesitated. Larten wouldn't want to hear this, but it wasn't the way of vampires to hide from the truth. "If he's an adult," Wester said slowly, "and he has grown up here, don't you think he'll have gone to fight in the trenches with all of the others his age?"

Larten's breath caught in his throat. He should have thought of that before, but it hadn't crossed his mind. He had been focused on Alicia. He only now gave any real thought to Gavner. The orphan had been a healthy child and Larten was sure he'd grown into a fit, able man. But many of the continent's finest young men had already perished on the fields of blood not too far from here. Was that why Alicia looked sad even when she was smiling?

210

"I have to find out," Larten said. "I cannot leave until I know."

"Very well," Wester said. "But we won't learn anything up here. Let's find somewhere to shelter from the sun. At dusk I'll visit more shops and inquire about the boy. I'm sure someone will be able to tell us what became of him."

But as Wester trailed from store to store that evening, he found that wasn't the case. Alicia had moved into her new home shortly before her daughter was born, and it had been only her and her husband. Nobody knew of any son. As far as the locals were aware, little Sylva was Alicia's only child.

Larten was frustrated and angry. He had never let himself get close to the boy, keeping Gavner at arm's length because he didn't feel entitled to any love from the child he had orphaned. But he felt more for Gavner than he would ever openly acknowledge or even admit to himself. He needed to know what had happened to the youth, especially as he saw this as a chance to play the part of a protective guardian. Gavner might have been taken prisoner. Maybe Larten could rescue him and lead him to safety the way he'd led the soldiers in no-man's-land. Or he might be lying ill in a hospital, waiting for medicine no human could provide in such a savage time, but that a vampire could locate. If Larten left now and later learned that he could have been of assistance...

Wester was one step ahead of his friend, as he often was, so the guard wasn't surprised when the General sighed and said that he couldn't leave. There was only one way to find out what had happened to Gavner, and Wester couldn't help him this time. Larten would have to face Alicia and question her himself.

Chapter Twenty-one

Larten approached the building boldly, as if he were one of the tenants. There weren't many people on the street at that time of night and those who saw him didn't spare him a second glance. He paused at the front door and made quick work of the lock, employing the skills he'd learned from a stage magician called Merletta many decades before. Once inside it was a simple case of following his nose—every person had a unique scent and even after so long apart he could have picked out Alicia's from a crowd of thousands.

He stood for a long time outside her door, afraid to knock. He had no idea how she might react. Would she scream, faint, attack him? Larten had faced many dangers in his life, but he'd seldom felt as nervous as he did that night.

Finally, knowing he'd never find the courage to face her if he didn't act now, he knocked three times and waited, removing his cap and scarf as he was standing there. It took Alicia a while to answer – it was late and she had been preparing for bed – but eventually she opened the door a crack and peered at him suspiciously. "Can I help you, monsieur?"

Larten realized that the corridor was darker than he'd thought. She couldn't see him properly. He took a step back so that the weak light illuminated his face.

Alicia drew a startled breath and the door creaked open another crack. She stared at him, eyes wide, wondering if she was dreaming. Larten said nothing, only let her study him. "It's really you?" she whispered.

"Aye," he said softly.

Alicia shivered when she heard his voice, then sighed and opened the door all the way. "I suppose you'd better come in then."

Larten looked around the room curiously when he entered. It wasn't as nicely decorated as their old apartment and there were far fewer ornaments. Some laundry was drying on a string by a window, something Alicia would never have allowed when he was living with her.

"Times change," she said, noting his surprise. "The war made light work of many a fortune. I'm no longer a woman of substance, though I still have more than many, plenty to get by on so long as things don't get any worse." She gestured to a chair and they sat opposite each other. Larten wasn't sure what to say, but luckily for him Alicia took the lead. "You look the same."

"We age slowly," Larten said. "One year for every ten that pass."

"You're talking about vampires?" she said softly and he nodded. "Then you're not ageless? According to the stories you live forever."

"As I tried to tell you when last we spoke, most of the stories are lies or distortions of the truth. We can live for hundreds of years, but we are mortal." He blushed. "You look the same too, as beautiful as ever."

Alicia winced and brushed back her hair with one hand. "That's sweet but untrue. This war has aged all of us. Sometimes I feel like a woman of sixty."

"No," Larten said firmly. "I would not say it if I did not mean it."

Alicia smiled at him, then shook her head miserably. Tears seeped from her eyes, almost breaking Larten's heart. "I've missed you, Vur," she moaned, and then she was hugging him hard, pressing herself against him as if afraid he was going to vanish on the cool night air.

It was long after midnight. The pair were still seated in the small living room, but on the same couch now, Alicia holding one of Larten's hands. They were sipping coffee – their third cup – and discussing their lives. Alicia had often thought of Larten and wondered about him. She regretted dismissing him before he'd had a chance to explain properly. She wished she hadn't acted so hastily.

Larten told her about life in the clan, the rules they followed, the way they fed, the laws they lived by. He was sorry he hadn't been honest with her when they first met. He thought she might have loved him regardless of his vampiric blood if he'd been true with her. Alicia hadn't banished him because he was a vampire, but because he'd lied.

She was worried when he told her about becoming a General. "Does that mean there's a vampire army?" she wanted to know.

"We are *gendarmes* more than anything else," he

said. "We exist to keep the members of the clan in order, not to wage war with any other."

When Alicia's thirst for knowledge about vampires had been sated, she told her story. The months after he'd left had been hard. People were gossiping about Vur Horston and she felt it was better to play along with the rumors rather than deny them. She put on a brave front and told her friends she'd dismissed him as soon as she realized he was one of the living dead.

"I told them you hadn't killed those women, but I said I had to get rid of you anyway—with a neck as long as mine, how could I sleep safely with a vampire?"

She continued to joke about it, and over time interest in the mysterious Vur Horston faded. Since Tanish had also left, she had no further contact with any of the people who'd been involved with Larten. She moved to a new apartment and did her best to forget about her lost fiancé.

"I met Jean some years later and we married after a short courtship. He was a kind man, no dark secrets. I didn't love him the same way I'd loved you, but I was happy. When we had Sylva, I was even happier."

"Is he involved in the war?" Larten asked when Alicia stalled.

"He was." She released Larten's hand and sighed. "Come and see Sylva."

She took Larten into a warm, brightly colored bedroom. Alicia's daughter was lying in a cot by the window. She was on her back and her left leg was cocked into the air. She was snoring lightly.

"Jean was a snorer," Alicia smiled. "All of the men in my life snored loudly—you, Jean..." She didn't mention Gavner. Larten noted the oversight – she'd hardly spoken of the boy at all – but he sensed that she had something else to tell him before talk turned to the orphan whom she'd adopted.

Alicia bent down Sylva's leg, then covered her with a soft blanket. "Jean was killed in battle almost a year ago," she whispered. If Larten hadn't been a vampire, he would have had to ask her to repeat it.

"None of your neighbors mentioned that," he murmured.

"They don't know." Alicia's eyes were brimming with tears. "So many women have lost husbands. I sometimes feel this is a city of widows. I don't want people staring at me sympathetically, rubbing Sylva's head and sighing, reminding her that her father is dead. She didn't know him well – she was little more than a baby when he died – and I'd rather spare her the news of his death until she's old enough to understand and deal with it."

"It must be hard bringing her up by yourself," Larten said softly.

"Yes," Alicia said. "But I manage. When this terrible war ends, I'll tell people Jean is dead and make a new life elsewhere, as I did when I lost my first true love. For the time being it's easier to pretend that all is well."

Larten smiled. "You would have made a good vampire."

She frowned. "Is that a compliment?"

"The highest I could pay." His smile faded—he couldn't hold back the question any longer. "And what of Gavner? What has become of your son?"

"*Our* son," she corrected him. When he scowled, she saw that time hadn't changed him in that regard. Sighing, she glanced one last time at the snoring Sylva, then led Larten back to the living room. This part of the story would enrage him and she didn't want him waking her daughter if he started to shout and curse.

"Gavner was distraught when you left." They were sitting on the couch and Alicia was holding his hand again. "I tried to explain, but how do you tell a boy that the man who raised him was a vampire? He missed Tanish as well, and was hurt by his abrupt disappearance. You were always rough with Gavner, but that was the first time Tanish had let him down."

"You should have told him Monsieur Eul was a murderer," Larten growled, his hatred for Tanish flaring again.

"I wish I had," Alicia said bitterly, surprising the vampire. "All was well for a time. Gavner dealt with his loss and excelled at school. He was never as close to me after that – I think he blamed me for the way you and Tanish abandoned him – but he still loved me. Then..."

Her voice cracked and Larten prepared himself for the worst. But when she went on, she didn't tell him that Gavner was dead. Her story was much darker than that.

"Tanish returned." Her features twisted. "He tried to woo me. He said he had always loved me, but hadn't dared court me while I was engaged to you. I told him I knew he was a killer, but he laughed that off and said I'd been misinformed. I wasn't fooled. I said I never wanted to see him again. I vowed to reveal his true identity if he stayed, and told him I'd left an incriminating document with a lawyer, to be opened in the event of my death."

"Was that a bluff?" Larten asked.

"No. I wrote a long letter, naming both of you and all that I knew about you, not long after you fled. I had a feeling I wasn't finished with the vampire partners." She smiled. "But I will go to my lawyer tomorrow and have your name removed."

"There is no need," Larten said. "I have little to do with humans. I doubt they can track me down at Vampire Mountain."

They both chuckled, then Alicia's face darkened again. "Gavner withdrew from me entirely. He came home late from school every evening, sometimes not until night. I suspected Tanish—he appeared to have left Paris, but I thought he was still here. I sent detectives to find him but without success. They couldn't keep track of Gavner either—he always managed to lose them, usually in a dark alley or tunnel.

"Then, one night, he never returned." She wiped tears from her cheeks and stared miserably at the wall. "That was the last I saw of him, and there has been no word since. Maybe it was nothing to do with Tanish. Perhaps he made other friends and ran away with one of them or died in a fight."

"But you do not think so," Larten said.

"No." She looked at him again. "I think that Tanish convinced him to become a vampire. I think he's one of your kind now. Except he doesn't have an honest, law-abiding master like you did. If I'm right, he's an assistant to a killer." Her hand tightened on Larten's and her eyes burned fiercely. "I asked you once not to harm Tanish Eul. Do you remember?"

"Aye," Larten said darkly.

Alicia squeezed even tighter. "I take that back. Find him, Vur. Kill him. And make that monster – that abductor of my child – *suffer* before you finish him off."

Chapter Twenty-two

Things could never be the way they had once been between Larten and Alicia, and there was no talk of them living together again or marrying. But the General stayed in Paris for a few months and the pair became close friends. Larten visited her every night. They talked about old times, the war, their hopes and fears for the future. They went for long walks, sometimes with Sylva. The girl liked Larten, but he was awkward around her. He had never been a natural with children, and although he tried to amuse her, he was too self-conscious to fully give himself over to play. Sylva didn't mind. She thought the stiff man with the strange way of talking was funny.

Wester remained in Paris, but kept out of their way. Larten wanted them to meet, but Wester felt he'd only complicate matters. "She met one of your vampire friends before and look how that turned out," he laughed whenever Larten pressed him. "This is your time. Enjoy it. We don't have to share *everything*."

Wester visited a few of the bars and casinos of Paris, but he didn't have much interest in them anymore. He spent most of his time in hospitals crammed full of wounded soldiers. He washed floors, carried patients from one room to another, helped in any way that he could. Wester no longer thought of himself as human, but despite that, he didn't like watching people suffer.

Larten would have happily stayed with Alicia until the end of the war, to make sure she got through it safely, but he couldn't stop thinking about Gavner. They hadn't discussed the boy since that first night. There was no need. Alicia had told Larten what she wanted, and she trusted him to take action when he was ready.

But time wasn't their ally. A rotten master could ruin a true-hearted assistant if you gave him long enough, and Tanish had already had several years to work on the boy and twist his view of the world.

Larten hoped to save Gavner and stop him from turning into a weak, selfish creature like Tanish, but if it wasn't already too late, it would be soon. If he didn't act swiftly, Gavner would be lost.

So, reluctantly, Larten took his leave. He bid Alicia farewell, and though it was a much sweeter parting than last time, his heart ached when he kissed her good-bye.

"Can I come see you again?" he asked.

"Whenever you please," Alicia smiled.

"My duties may take me to far-off places for long stretches," he told her. "But when I can, I will find you and visit for a while."

"You can watch me grow old," Alicia laughed.

"I would like that," Larten said seriously, then sighed. "If I do not return, you will know that something has happened to me. As long as I am alive, I will come back. If I do not come..."

She pressed a finger to his lips. "No talk of gloomy matters," she chided him, then asked him to give Sylva one last ride on his back before he went.

The journey to Vampire Mountain passed uneventfully. Both vampires were looking forward to their return, especially Wester. He had meant to explore the world for a few more years, but when Larten said he had to go back, Wester agreed to accompany him without a moment's hesitation. He had missed the Halls more than he'd thought he would. He felt out of place everywhere else. He didn't think he'd ever again leave the mountain for a lengthy period of time, unless a Prince or a close friend asked it of him.

There were more vampires present than either had expected and there was a buzz of excitement in the cool air of the Halls and tunnels. They soon learned that Mika Ver Leth had been summoned by Paris Skyle. According to the rumors, Paris was going to nominate the young General to become a Prince. If that was true, and a majority of the Princes approved, the rest of the clan would need to be consulted over the coming years before a vote could be tallied. But those who'd heard had come as fast as they could.

Nominations were rare. Sometimes the clan could go hundreds of years without a new Prince being appointed. But the older Princes were dying off after a long reign, and this was a time of great change. First Vancha had been invested, and now the even younger and less experienced Mika was in the frame. Nobody within easy traveling distance of Vampire

Mountain wanted to miss what might prove to be a pivotal moment in the clan's history.

"You have a great sense of timing," Vancha laughed when he found Wester and Larten in the Hall of Khledon Lurt. They were sitting with their old master, Seba Nile, and like everybody else they were talking about Mika Ver Leth. Vancha sat on the bench beside Wester. A subdued-looking Arrow – he had been walking with Vancha – sat next to Larten.

"Who told you about Mika?" Vancha asked.

"Nobody," Larten said. "We only heard about it when we arrived. Is it true that Paris plans to nominate him?"

Vancha shrugged, spat into a bowl of bat broth, then drained it with one long swallow. "Paris doesn't need to discuss such matters with me."

"But I imagine that he would have," Larten pressed.

"Maybe," Vancha grinned. "But if he did, I'm keeping it to myself. I don't want to spoil the surprise for everyone."

"It will mean a huge adjustment for the clan if it is true," Seba said. "Mika will be very different than any other Prince of recent times. You and he would make quite a contrasting pair, Sire."

"Contrast can be good," Vancha grunted.

"I think it can be *very* good," Seba said approvingly.

"But sometimes an even stronger contrast is required," Wester muttered and the others looked at him with surprise.

"You don't like Mika?" Vancha frowned.

Wester shrugged. "I don't really know him. He seems like an honorable man from what I've seen. But we need a different type of Prince. Mika will serve the clan capably, I'm sure, but he won't introduce sweeping changes."

"Do we need sweeping changes?" Vancha asked.

"Yes." Wester's eyes had the hard look he got whenever talk swung around to the vampaneze and Larten knew where this was heading. "There's a time for moderate leaders, but this isn't it. Mika would have made a fine Prince a hundred years ago and maybe he'll make a fine Prince a century from now. But at this moment we should be looking for revolutionary, innovative Princes."

"A Prince who'll give you what you want," Vancha said softly. "But not what you necessarily need."

"We're not children," Wester growled. "We should be given the chance to decide what we need."

"You're given that chance every time a Prince is nominated," Vancha argued. "If enough of you vote against Mika – assuming he gets nominated – the Princes will think long and hard about his rejection and perhaps put forward a General more likely to advocate war. That's what you hunger for, isn't it?"

Wester said nothing, afraid that he might anger Vancha.

"Princes are not chosen to bend to the wishes of the clan," Seba said calmly. "We look for different qualities at different times, but the most important measures of a Prince are constant. They must be loyal, honest, brave, intelligent, true. They should embody all that a vampire of good standing wishes to be.

"If Paris nominates Mika, it will be because he sees those qualities in him, not because he wishes to lead the clan in a certain direction." Seba laid a hand on Wester's arm. "I know you hate the vampaneze and would like to see us led into war with our blood-cousins. But you should not seek to have a General nominated simply because he shares your beliefs, or vote against one purely because he does not. Humans elect leaders on the basis of the promises they make. We try to elect ours based solely on the strength of their character."

"Of course." Wester smiled, but his smile was strained and Larten could tell he didn't agree with their old master. He thought about contributing to the debate, but before he could say anything a young vampire at the table next to theirs spoke up.

"Forgive me for interrupting, but I overheard what you were saying and I'd like to know why you hate the vampaneze so much."

Larten looked around and found a thin, blond vampire in a light blue shirt. He was smiling warmly.

"What's not to hate?" Wester snapped. "They betrayed the clan and killed many of us in the war. They're murderers."

"But *we* started the war," the young vampire said, moving across to join them, not overawed by the fact that he was sharing a table with a Prince and the highly respected quartermaster of Vampire Mountain. "The vampaneze only wanted the freedom to lead their own lives. They never threatened the clan or undermined the rule of the Princes."

"You think so?" Wester hooted. His face lit up as he warmed to the challenge. He didn't mind vampires who argued with him. There was always a chance you could swing a man's opinion if you both talked freely. Wester was only frustrated by those who kept their own council, like the close-lipped Larten. "What's your name, youngster?"

"Kurda Smahlt," the fresh-faced vampire said.

"Well, listen closely, Kurda, while I tell you *precisely* why we have to be wary of the vampaneze."

Larten hid a smile as Wester launched into a long list of reasons, each of which the younger vampire calmly refuted. After a while he began to think that Wester had met his match — Kurda was as set in his ways as Wester was, and Larten suspected that the pair would have many arguments like this over the years to come.

Larten was pleased to note Arrow's neutral position as Wester and Kurda batted the problem of the vampaneze back and forth. He listened intently, but with a troubled expression. Vancha had obviously managed to soothe his friend since Larten had last seen him, and while Arrow would always despise their purple-skinned enemies, Larten didn't think that hatred would consume him or drive him as it drove Wester.

As the argument entered its third hour – more vampires had joined them and the table was getting overcrowded – Larten excused himself and cocked an eyebrow at Vancha, letting him know that he wanted to speak to the Prince in private. When they were out of earshot, he asked if Vancha would be staying until Mika arrived.

"I planned to hang around awhile," Vancha said cautiously, not giving much away. "Why?"

"I have need of a friend," Larten replied. "I will be leaving Vampire Mountain tomorrow and I hoped you would come with me."

"Leaving already?" Vancha sniffed. "It's not because of that girl, is it—Arra Sails, Mika's assistant? You were sweet on her, aye?"

Larten blinked. "How do you know that?"

"They didn't make me a Prince just because of my dashing good looks," Vancha chuckled.

Larten smiled, then grew serious. "This has nothing to do with Arra or Mika. I must attend to personal business. But it is the business of the Princes too, which is why I am asking for your help."

Vancha listened silently as Larten explained. When he was done, Vancha bowed and said, "You are a true vampire and it will be an honor to accompany you."

"What about Mika?" Larten asked.

Vancha smiled. "Between you and me, Paris *is* going to nominate him, but I've already given my vote of confidence. I don't need to be here. Let's go check the Stone of Blood and take to the road at sunset." He spat on the floor and winked. "It will be good to be back in the open. This damn mountain isn't big enough to hold the likes of Vancha March!"

Chapter Twenty-three

Petrograd was a volatile city. It had been the Russian capital until recently, the eye of the revolutionary storm that had torn apart the grand old country. There was an uncertain desperation in the air—nobody knew whether the state would flourish, what the future held, how safe their children would be. Murder, gambling and vice were rife. It was as if the city had been created especially for men of dark, self-serving greed. Men like Tanish Eul.

They could have triangulated the search with Paris Skyle's help, but Larten didn't need the Stone of Blood for this section of the hunt. Once the Stone had revealed the prodigal's approximate location, it was a simple matter to do the rounds of casinos and houses of ill repute once they reached the city.

They found Tanish on the second night. He was surrounded by scores of *pretty things*, women who had to smile at the obscene likes of Tanish Eul or starve. Larten could see loathing in the eyes of those who swarmed around Tanish, but the fat, finely dressed vampire didn't seem to notice. He patted the women like pets, tipped the croupiers and doormen who sneered when his back was turned, and acted as if he were the most loved man in Petrograd.

Only one person looked at Tanish with genuine fondness. That was a young, brown-haired man. He wasn't very tall, but he was broad, with a wide smile and slightly yellow teeth. He tried to steer Tanish away from those who would happily stick a knife in his back. When the vampire dropped coins, the younger man scurried to beat the *pretty things* to them, and returned those he rescued from the floor. He watered down Tanish's wine when the vampire was distracted. And at the end of the night he carefully guided the older man back to their hotel.

"Whatever else, he's a faithful assistant," Vancha murmured as they watched the lights go out in the huge set of rooms that Tanish and Gavner shared.

Larten didn't respond. It had pained him to watch Gavner Purl play servant to so vile a master as Tanish Eul. Gavner had grown since Larten last saw him, but he was all too recognizable. There were dark rims around his eyes – evidence of too many parties and marathon gambling sessions – but his face hadn't changed much. When Larten looked at him, he saw the boy he'd brought back from Greenland, and his heart ached to see that child come to such a wretched position as this.

"Will we go in?" Vancha asked as the dawn sun rose behind them.

"No," Larten said. "I want him to be sober when I face him."

"That could be a long wait," Vancha huffed, but he retired along with Larten. This was the General's quest, not his, and the Prince was content to follow the younger vampire's lead.

They waited for Tanish and Gavner on the roof of their hotel. When the pair emerged a few hours after sunset, the Prince and General trailed them from the rooftops. They kept their distance until Tanish turned down a long, narrow alley, then Vancha raced ahead to the far end. Larten let the pair on the ground advance halfway. Then, gathering his red cloak about him, he stepped forward and dropped.

Tanish yelped as the red figure landed in the path ahead of him. Gavner was instantly in front of his master, a knife in his hand, protecting the man he thought of as a father.

"Back!" Gavner barked.

"Easy, my boy," Tanish muttered. "It might be someone who accidentally fell. Let's have a good look at..."

Tanish's eyes widened as Larten stood. The obese vampire had often dreamed of this moment. The first few years of exile had been awful. He was convinced that Larten would hunt him down and butcher him. Again, when he'd wheedled Gavner away from Alicia, he was sure that the orange-haired vampire would come seeking revenge. But as the years passed, he came to believe that Larten had either been killed or had lost interest in him. Now he saw what a fool he'd been.

"Vur Horston!" Gavner gasped, his face whitening. He and Tanish had never discussed the scarred man of mystery who'd raised him—Vur was a forbidden topic of conversation as far as Tanish was concerned. Gavner had often wondered about the orange-haired, solemn man and what he'd do if they ever came face-to-face again. But now that the central figure from his past was in front of him, he didn't know how to react.

"Stand aside, Gavner Purl," Larten said, addressing him the same rough way he had when Gavner was a boy.

"No!" Tanish squealed, clutching Gavner's jacket. "Don't leave me!"

"I'm not going anywhere," Gavner growled, pointing his knife at their assailant. "Back off or I'll–"

Larten moved like a bolt of lightning. Gavner had been blooded, and his vision was sharper than any human's, but even so he couldn't follow the vampire's movements. It was as if the red-cloaked man momentarily disappeared then reappeared in the same position as before. Gavner felt a stinging blow to his wrist and when he glanced down, his knife was gone.

Gavner squinted and spotted his knife in Larten's hand. The General dropped the blade and said, "Gavner. Please. Step aside. You have been misled and misinformed. This man is a charlatan. He has disobeyed the laws of the clan. You owe him no allegiance and it will go badly for you if you try to defend him."

"*Clan?*" Gavner muttered.

"The vampire clan," Larten said.

"You're a vampire too?" Gavner asked.

"Aye."

"And there are more of you?"

"Of course. You thought that you and Tanish were the only two?"

"No. But he never said anything about the others. I thought maybe a handful or a few dozen…"

"There are thousands of us," Larten said. "And we live by strict laws. Tanish has broken those laws and must pay the price. Now step aside before–"

"No!" Tanish screamed, grabbing Gavner's arm, eyes bulging. "He'll kill me!"

"No he won't," Gavner said savagely. "I won't let him."

"You are loyal," Larten noted. "That is admirable. But your loyalty has been misplaced. This piece of scum is not worthy of it."

"Watch your mouth," Gavner snarled. "Tanish has been more of a father to me than you ever were. If you try to hurt him, you'll have to fight me first."

Larten nodded, then looked over Gavner's shoulder at the trembling Tanish Eul. "I think you took

Gavner because you loved him," Larten said softly. "If so, would you see him killed now?"

"You won't harm him," Tanish moaned. "He's your boy as much as he's mine. You wouldn't–"

"I will do what a General must!" Larten thundered. "I am here for you, Tanish Eul, and if I have to kill Gavner to get to you, I will." His face softened. "But I do not think you will force me to do that. There is not much goodness left in you, but I refuse to believe that you have sunk so low that you will see Gavner slaughtered just so that you can enjoy an extra few minutes of life. He can be spared, but only if you have the courage to face me on your own, as you swore you would when we last parted."

"Don't listen to him," Gavner said. "I'll stand by you, no matter what."

"No," Tanish sighed and took a step away. Gavner frowned, confused. Tanish was sweating and shaking, but he moved ahead of his assistant and faced Larten directly. "This is between you and me. Gavner's innocent. Will you give me your word that you won't harm him?"

"I will," Larten said.

"Master! No!" Gavner shouted.

"Peace," Tanish smiled, glancing over his shoulder. "There is much I never told you about myself and the clan, much that this good General will reveal when I am...indisposed." He chuckled sickly, then glared at Gavner. "And he *is* good. Don't hate him and don't attack him, not until you've heard him out. You might not think so fondly of me once he informs you of all the facts."

"I don't want to listen to him," Gavner yelled. "I don't care what he has to say. It won't make any difference."

"Not even if he tells you that I'm a killer?" Tanish asked quietly.

Gavner's mouth fell open. "No..." he whispered.

"Aye," Tanish said grimly. "I'm a man of many weaknesses. You know that better than most, and you have overlooked them all, for which I will be eternally grateful. But I hid my vilest crimes from you. I murdered an innocent woman and allowed others to be butchered when I had the power to spare their lives. Not even you can forgive me that, can you?"

Gavner gulped. "It can't be true."

Tanish said, "It is."

"You would never have..." Gavner moaned.

"I did."

"There must have been a reason," Gavner whispered.

"Only this—I sacrificed them to save my own life."

Tears of pain and frustration filled Gavner's eyes. Tanish smiled lovingly at the young man and blinked back his own tears. "As weak and self-serving as I was," Tanish mumbled, "I only ever wanted the best for you. I love you like a son and always will, even while my soul rots for all eternity, as it most surely shall." Tanish half-saluted Gavner, then faced Larten again and steeled himself. "Go on. Get it over with. I won't try to stop you."

"I did not come here to execute you," Larten said. "I will afford you a fair opportunity to save yourself, which is more than you ever gave Ginette or any of the others. Fight me, Tanish, as you said you would, and if you get the better of me, you can live."

Tanish gulped and shook his head. "No," he wheezed.

"You must," Larten growled. "If you do not accept my challenge, you will die for certain. This way you have a chance."

"I don't have any *chance*," Tanish jeered. "You're a General at the height of your powers, while I'm a fat, faded fool. I've seen you in action, Quicksilver, and we both know you're far too sharp for me. This is an execution, plain and simple. Kill me if you must, but don't pretend that I ever had any real hope of protecting myself."

"Only a coward would let himself be slaughtered like this," Larten hissed.

"I never claimed to be anything else," Tanish said softly.

Larten was disappointed, but not surprised. He had anticipated this and planned for it. Stepping forward, he pressed a nail to Tanish's fleshy throat, pricked the skin, drew a few drops of blood...then moved aside and lowered his hand.

"Go," Larten said. "Leave and never let me see you again."

Tanish blinked, bewildered. "This is a trick," he whispered.

"Go," Larten repeated, firmly this time.

"What about Gavner? Will you—"

Larten raised a finger and pointed it at Tanish's heart. The oversized vampire didn't need any further

warning. With a miserable last glance at the astonished, agonized Gavner Purl, he lurched away from
his assistant and his old friend, sobbing with relief
and sadness as he was swallowed by the shadows of
the alley.

There was a long silence as Gavner watched his
master, the closest thing he'd ever had to a father,
stumble away in disgrace. The young man's mind
was spinning. He wanted to rush after Tanish and
tell him he didn't care about his sins, that he wanted
to be his assistant – his son – forever. He took a shaky
step forward, but was stopped by the vampire in the
red clothes.

"Wait," Larten said quietly.

That single word alerted Gavner to the danger.
He realized that Tanish was right—his release *was*
just a trick. Gavner opened his mouth to shout a
warning, but before he could, there came a short,
startled cry from the far end of the alley.

Then silence.

"What have you done?" Gavner cried.

"He was a killer," Larten replied calmly. "The
clan demands the death of those who kill without
just cause. It was not in my power to set him free.

Another was waiting to dispatch him. But at least he died thinking freedom was in his grasp. That was better than facing death honestly. Tanish never had much time for honesty."

"You murdered him!" Gavner shouted, hands bunched into fists, eyes glittering with angry tears.

"I sent him to his death," Larten said. "But I suppose from a certain point of view that is one and the same thing."

"I'll kill you," Gavner wept. "If you don't deal with me tonight, I'll track you down and make you pay for what you did to Tanish. I don't care how long it takes."

"You will not have to wait," Larten said. He retrieved the knife he had cast aside earlier and pressed it into Gavner's hand. As Gavner stared with shock at the cold metal, the elder creature of the night said, "My name is Larten Crepsley. I am a vampire General. Tanish Eul was executed for good reason and I do not apologize for that.

"But I also slaughtered your real mother and father. In a moment of mad rage, I took their lives and left you an orphan. If you choose to take my life as payment for theirs, you will be within your rights and no vampire will hold it against you.

246

"Pass judgment on me, Gavner Purl, and let your hand rise or fall as destiny decides it must."

With that, Larten knelt in the muddy filth of the Petrograd alley, offered his throat and calmly waited for the stunned, uncertain Gavner to spare his life or kill him as he saw fit.

To be continued...

Dying to find out how Larten Crepsley ends up
at the Cirque Du Freak? It won't be a pretty tale.
The Saga of Larten Crepsley concludes with
Brothers to the Death!

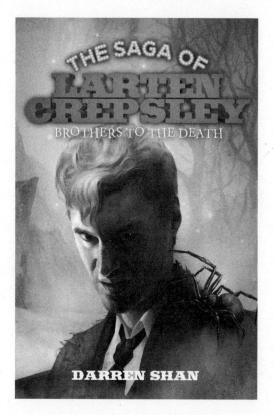

Turn the page for a sneak peek.

Available now.

On a grassy bank in a park on the outskirts of Paris, a young man lay beside a middle-aged woman, holding her hand. They were talking softly, shielded from the setting evening sun by a large umbrella. Those passing by thought they were perhaps a mother and son. None suspected that the orange-haired gentleman in the blood-red suit was more than twice the age of the woman.

"What do you think people would say if I kissed you?" Larten murmured.

Alicia giggled. "There would be a scandal." Much about her had changed over the years, but her giggle was the same as ever.

"I relish a juicy scandal," Larten said, leaning closer towards her.

"Don't!" Alicia laughed, pushing him away. "You know I don't like it when you tease me."

"What if I was not teasing?" Larten asked with a smile. But the smile was for Alicia's benefit. He was serious—he *did* want to kiss her.

"That's sweet of you," Alicia said. "But I'm an old woman. You can't have any real interest in me after all these decades. I'm a wrinkly hag!"

"Hardly," Larten snorted. Alicia looked much older than him now, but in his eyes she was as beautiful as when they'd first met almost thirty years earlier.

Alicia rolled away from him, into the sunlight, where she stretched and lazily studied the clouds. Larten's smile never faltered, but inside he felt sad. It had been a decade and a half since his reunion with Alicia. They had met often over the course of those years. Each time he hoped she'd kiss him, declare her love for him, accept him as her husband. He wanted things to be like they were in 1906, when they were engaged and madly in love.

But Alicia felt that she was too old to marry again, and if she ever did give her hand to another man, she wanted to give it to a man her own age. It didn't matter that Larten had been born almost eighty years before her. He looked like he was in his twenties and that was how she thought of him. To Alicia he could never be more than a friend. Larten had accepted that—he had no choice—but he couldn't help wishing he was more.

"The children are having fun," Alicia noted, nodding at a boy and girl playing by the edge of a small pond.

The girl was almost eighteen, a young woman who would probably marry soon and have children of her own. But Larten still thought of her as little Sylva. She was a tall, slim, pretty maid, but to him she would always be a cute, chubby baby.

The *boy* was in his thirties but didn't look much older than Sylva. He was a vampire like Larten, aging only one year for every ten that passed. He was of medium height, but broad, built like a wrestler. He could have thrown Sylva to the far side of the pond, but he always handled her gently, as Larten had taught him, careful never to squeeze too hard when he was holding her hand, knowing he could shatter every bone in her fingers if he did.

Gavner hadn't wanted to return to Paris. He had left under a cloud, swearing loyalty to Tanish Eul, a weak, selfish vampire who had killed an innocent woman to save his own thickly layered neck. When Larten caught up with them and herded the killer to his execution, Gavner thought his world had ended. He hated the man whom he'd known since childhood as Vur Horston, and yearned to strike him dead.

Larten had granted him that opportunity. Handing Gavner a knife, the General told him that he had killed Gavner's parents. He said that Gavner had every right to exact revenge, and he offered himself to the bewildered teenager.

Gavner would never forget how close he'd come to stabbing Larten. His mind was in a whirl. Tanish Eul's sudden death had shocked him. When he learned that Larten had killed his parents too, it seemed like the only way to end the madness was to murder the orange-haired vampire. His fingers tightened and he tried to drive the knife forward into Larten's heart, stopping it forever.

But something held him back. He still wasn't sure why he hadn't struck. Maybe it had been the calm acceptance in Larten's eyes, the fact that he wasn't afraid of death, that he felt like he deserved to die. Perhaps it was because the vampire had been true to him for the first time in his life, and Gavner couldn't kill a man for telling the truth. Or maybe he just didn't have a killer's instinct.

Whatever the reason, Gavner had let the knife drop, collapsed in a weeping huddle, and given himself over to confusion and grief.

"I wish you could spend more time with us," Alicia sighed as Gavner chased Sylva around the pond, threatening to throw her in. "Sylva misses you when you're not here."

"I suspect she misses Gavner more," Larten remarked wryly. He had never been much of a father figure. He'd always been distant with Sylva, and especially with Gavner. It was a mystery to him why the pair liked him so much.

"Gavner's like a brother to her," Alicia admitted, "but she's fond of you too. She thinks of you as an uncle."

"*Uncle Larten*," the vampire chuckled, blushing slightly. "How ridiculous."

"Don't be so stuffy," Alicia growled, pinching his left cheek until his scar burned whitely. Then she smiled and kissed one of her fingers and pressed it to the scar. "You still haven't told me how you got that," she said, changing the subject.

"I will one night," Larten promised. "When you are old enough."

The pair laughed. Gavner heard the laughter—his senses were much sharper than a human's—and he paused to smile in the direction of the couple who had been the only real parents he'd ever known. (He tried not to think about the nights when he had served as Tanish Eul's surrogate son. While he would never speak ill of Tanish, who had been nothing but loving to Gavner, he was ashamed that he had not seen through the killer's mask.)

Larten and Vancha March had helped Gavner recover. They'd told him much about the clan, explained Tanish's bitter history, helped prepare him for life as a creature of the night. When they left Petrograd, Larten urged Gavner to travel with Vancha. He said that the Prince could teach Gavner more than he ever could. But Gavner asked to learn from Larten instead. He had always wanted to get closer to the aloof, tall man with the scar. He saw this as a chance to gain a father. There were no more lies between them. He hoped to build a strong relationship with Larten Crepsley, to earn his respect and love.

Larten did respect Gavner, and loved him in his own strange way. But he never made any open display of affection. He was shy with most people, slow to reveal anything personal. But it went beyond shyness with Gavner. He had orphaned the boy and would never allow himself to forget that. He had told Gavner the whole sad story, how he'd been suffering with a fever, how his young assistant had been killed, the way he'd lost his mind and slaughtered a shipful of humans.

Gavner had forgiven him—he had come close to killing when he lost Tanish Eul, so he could empathize with the older vampire—but Larten still blamed himself, and every time he looked at Gavner he was reminded of that dark day, of the stain on his soul. Though he had spent most of the last fifteen years with the youth, teaching him the ways of the clan, he'd always kept his assistant at arm's length, insisting Gavner treat him as nothing more than a tutor.

"I will never be a father to you," he'd declared several years ago, after Gavner had absentmindedly referred to Larten as his father. "I do not deserve such love and I will cast you aside if you ever speak of me in that way again. I will accept your friendship if you feel I am entitled to it, but no more than that."

Gavner knew that Larten thought of him as more than a mere assistant, just as he thought of Larten as more than a mentor. But he accepted the older vampire's rules and never again spoke of his true feelings. If this was what Larten needed in order to feel comfortable around his student and would-be son, so be it. He would do anything to please the man who had reluctantly reared him.

While Gavner studied Larten and Alicia, smiling sadly as he thought of the past, Sylva snuck up on him and pushed him hard. Gavner yelped, arms flailing, then fell into the water. He came up spluttering and roaring. He looked for Sylva, to drag her in, but she'd already fled—she knew how swiftly a vampire could react.

"Hide me!" Sylva squealed, seeking shelter behind her mother and Larten.

"If you were my daughter I would spank you," Larten growled as Gavner hauled himself out of the pond. "You know that sunlight is bad for him. I will have to help him fish his hat out of the pond before his hair catches fire."

Sylva's smile faded as she stared at the glowering vampire. But then Larten winked and she knew that everything was fine. She looked on with delight as he hurried to the shivering Gavner, expressing concern for him—then howled with glee as he shoved his unsuspecting assistant back into the pond.

"Men never grow up," Alicia tutted, but she was smiling too. She offered Gavner the rug she was sitting on when they returned, and helped him dry his hair. She corrected him when he cursed Larten and Sylva—"Gentlemen do not use such crude words."—then packed up and led them home.

Gavner and Sylva strayed ahead of their elders, walking arm in arm. Sylva chatted about friends, fashion, and movies, and Gavner pretended to be interested in such things. He had already forgiven her for pushing him into the pond—he'd never been one to hold a grudge. Larten and Alicia followed leisurely, strolling like any ordinary couple.

"How long can you stay this time?" Alicia asked, already knowing the answer. Larten and Gavner had arrived a week earlier, and though nothing had been said, she'd gathered within a few hours that it would be a short visit. Larten always tried to cram in a lot if he wasn't staying long. When she heard him making plans for all the things that he wanted to do, she knew the pair would be moving on in a matter of days, not weeks or months. From his expression this afternoon, she realized the time had come for them to leave, so she asked the question at last, the same way she always did. It was a long-established routine of theirs.

"We go tonight," Larten said. "We have a meeting that we must attend. It is not far from here as vampires measure things, but it will take us most of the night to get there."

"Will you return soon?" she asked, again already knowing the answer.

Larten sighed. "I do not think so. We have been forced to deal with unpleasant but determined people, and I suspect the negotiations will take some time."

"How mysterious your lives are," Alicia said enviously. "I bet you're off to meet a magician or witch."

"Nothing so fanciful," Larten smiled. "I would prefer it if we were. These men pose more of a threat to the world, I fear, than any being of magic."

"What do you mean?" Alicia asked, frowning at him as they reached the small house where she and Sylva lived.

"We do not have much to do with human politicians or soldiers," Larten said, pausing at the door to cast one last glance at the setting sun. "But occasionally a group tries to forge links with us and we find ourselves having to deal with them. This is one such time, and I am worried about the outcome. Tell me, Alicia, what do you know about *Nazis*?"